I0742010

*Nastya Valentine's*

# Ultimate Fantasy

ISBN: 979-8-9920663-3-3
Catalog Number: DBBC015

Dream Boy Book Club
dreamboybook.club
USA

# Table of Contents

# *Introduction: Pre-Everything*

I wrote this series of eroto-philosophical fantasies to explore deep desires I have within myself; at the site of heartbreak, I have encountered inspiration and alchemized pain into fantasy. A trilogy of alternate realities, each containing elements of an elusive, unhinged desire. Feelings of regret, a despondence of not having, and yet the relief of gratitude of not having. The grass is always greener in someone else's garden. Irreconcilable dualities: to at once live and not live a certain life. An alternate reality can be an ultimate fantasy, or a worst nightmare.

The first alternate reality presents the scenario of a traditional life path: marriage, husband, house, children, the life of a stay at home mom. She has the perfect life, or so it all seems, until a rendezvous with a man from her past disrupts her picture perfect serenity. This was inspired by a real life breakup, and the idea to write a story out of this came to me when he said "I'll be here when you want to cheat on your sugar daddy husband with the pool boy." Damn my vivid imagination – yes, I had already imagined this. From the end of September to the end of December, I worked on this anthology. A fertile season, by any means.

The second alternate reality presents the opposite scenario, a life path that hasn't been seen as traditional but is now the norm: an ambitious, goal-oriented career woman. She doesn't need anybody, she got herself always, and this independent attitude threatens her relationship. At a breaking point at home, but a high point at work, she has a life changing encounter with a woman who comes on to her at a party – challenging her beliefs of strength and fragileness. This is the scenario opposite to the first one, where I switch places with the male SO, and is an expansion of the Christina character from my 2019 drama film Zero Illumination (which was inspired by another real life breakup).

The third alternate reality presents a nonhuman point of view: rather, an artificial intelligence program coded into a robotic female body, undergoing a process that grants her human consciousness. Having spent most of her existence fighting and being hunted, her world is fundamentally altered after falling from a building – only to crawl away into the house of a man who can help her survive. The Lattice communication device, and the program Clarence, are again self-referential, from my ambient scifi film Princess on Vacation, my first appearance nude on camera.

Adding a dimension of erotica to this anthology was a natural progression: with my experiences in sex work, the Cyberhorny book, and fantastical dream explorations, the dovetailing of sexuality and writing is a blessed union.

These three narratives intertwine, as they have a common universe within them. A multitude of perspectives, frames of reference from whence I look at the world.

Does this author want to be a tradwife? Absolutely. Hell yeah. But as modernity is the new tradition, taking a trad path is frowned upon. Even fantasizing, thinking about it is shameful: many people now want to retire the social clock.

"But you are so non-traditional, you are so unique and unorthodox," many people tell me. Two things can exist at once – I can have a ☆ weird ☆ career path, (out of necessity rather than choice), and I can have a trad desire that harkens the social clocks many women would rather outdate.

But as a woman living my own prism of subjective experience, my own prison of femininity, a beautiful gorgeous stunning fertile woman, the biological visceral body quarrels with the intangible conceptual social construct. The biological clock is one that cannot be retired. As I get older, as fertility slips from my grasp, time being tepid sinkwater through my talon manicured hands, I yearn deeper for concepts I've rejected in the past. A Jungian enantiodromia.

If there is an error in the programming of my heart, I take it upon myself to do the troubleshooting.

Has this author fallen off a building and revived herself robotically while crawling through dark streets at night? Certainly not, but the pain I have felt from relying on only myself in life makes me crave a type of de-sentience.

A robotic, tradwifelife subservience where someone else can take care of life's burdens for me, for I am fully exhausted. Situations to create this fantasy of subservience become more extreme: first an obedient wife; then a sexually submissive woman plied into relinquishing control at a ritualistic sex party; lastly, a programmed machine falling off a building. All three women, in some form, have to obey. There is a tension between complying and disobeying, the push and pull towards traditional values or progressive futures.

This anthology delves into themes of bountiful fertility, drama, PAIN, tradition vs modernity, the fragileness of human emotion, artificial replication of consciousness, duplicity, and delusions of convenience. Sometimes we have to convince ourselves of one thing simply because we cannot believe the other.

As always, I include elements from the drama of my real life into the drama of fiction. While I may not have lived through all of these situations, I certainly mined the blockchain of lived experience to be my muse.

Pain remains exiguous. What makes a woman? Fertility and pain.

"I'm a different kind of woman. If you want a basic bitch, go to the Beverly Center."

Lana Del Rey

# Proof of Life

**Mommy**

If anything can happen, it might.

Kids with husband. Mansion in Brentwood. I have everything I could ever want. My husband is always busy. He has an incredibly demanding C-suite biotech job that makes this all possible.

While I don't exactly know the ins and outs of his work life, I know it's a series of highly classified cutting edge projects that have only gotten more demanding over time. He's at home less and less, business trips are frequent and NDAs signed by his employees make it impenetrable to discuss. When he tells me about his work, I listen, but much of the jargon is beyond my understanding. I remain impressed, day by day, waiting up for him if he comes home late, waiting up for him dutifully if he's just come home from a three day, four day, fourteen day business trip, giving him a kiss and telling him, "kids are asleep, sheets are changed, I love this silk but I love being wrapped up in your arms even more."

"You're the best," he strokes my hair, wistfully twirling an auburn strand. I'd greet him in the foyer and walk him into the kitchen, where the dinner I prepared is waiting.

"The red looks good on you."

"What about this red?" I slip off my modal grey Lise Charmel robe to reveal a dainty scarlet Agent Provocateur lingerie set. A lace bra with delicate latex straps, pushing up my newly D cup mommy tits, curves filling out my my red hot outfit, not flat as a board in skinnylicious days past. A matching garter belt over my hourglass milf hips, molten hot red lava on the panties clinging to my round ass.

"Does this red look good too?"

"Fuck, you're a vision," his stare devours me, ignoring the swordfish I'd cooked earlier sitting on the marble counter. I served him me, on a silver platter.

"I should come home more often."
"I'll be waiting for you like this every time."

He'd come home from a business trip to me disrobing into red Agent Provocateur, pale blue Kiki Montparnasse, neon yellow Honey Birdette, deep green Edge o Beyond, nymph pink Studio Pia – sultry sets I'd buy with his black card for the pleasure of watching him take it all in. A rainbow of five star main courses. Mommy's still got it. And Daddy gets to have it.

HUSBAND HAMBURGERS
1 swordfish steak, cooked til crispy
1 buns, toasted lightly
2 leaves of lettuce
2 sheets of nori
3 sliced tomatoes
¼ spoon soy ginger glaze
⅔ spoon oil

A simple fish-based burger made in just fifteen minutes! Cook fishsteak in pan or air fryer, use EXTRA VIRGIN olive oil to give it that delightful sizzle. Toast buns for 2 minutes so that they're loyal and devoted, and whisper your marriage vows into the lettuce and tomatoes as they harmonize within the burger. Serve on 2 sheets of nori laid flat on a large white porcelain plate, symbolizing the marital beds for a delicious eternity together. ♡

As his business grew more and more demanding, projects requiring more energy and time, clandestine operations draining his brain, our personal clandestine operations left less availability for me to drain his balls.

"I'm so exhausted, baby, can we cuddle up and pass out?"
"Of course."
"Thank you for being so sexy. I love you."
And lights out.

He closes his deep blue eyes, and falls asleep when his head hits the pillow, still grinning. Despite the growing appearance of under eye bags and wrinkles, he looks handsome, peaceful, happy. Knowing that I'm the cause of this little daily peacefulness, the first thing he sees in the morning and the last before the night ends, makes me happy in a way I've never imagined. So I stroke his slicked back black hair, run my hands through the threads of greys above his high forehead, tap his cheekbone gently, and give him a kiss goodnight before rolling over and settling into my own cozy corner of the bed.

I think about what I have to do the next day, how I want to spend my time.

I'm responsible for what goes on in the house. We have a part time maid, nanny, and chef, a very small staff, but I insist on doing as much as I can myself, keeping the place clean, the food delicious, and the children occupied. LaTesla Grace and DarkJulian are in daycare, a prestigious private facility their nanny takes them to from 8am to 6pm every weekday. They love Miss Ava, but I still tuck them in at night.

Most of our days are like this. He holds it down at work, I hold it down at home. He is the provider, I am the nurturer.

I've deeply longed for this dynamic as long as I have known, and consider myself incredibly blessed and lucky. The slowness of life, the mundaneness, the ordinariness of the day to day – it's not boring. It's stable as a horse grazing in the hay. I love this boredom.

When there've been times in life where I couldn't handle one more nervous breakdown, the intensity of chaoticness, I'll take boring over exciting any day.

One day, a day like any other, my idyllic boredom was disrupted.

♥

5AM, a summer Monday, my husband and I wake up in the morning and share a kiss. We cuddle. We roll out of the silk-cocooned California King bed and brush our teeth in the double-sinked master bathroom. He gets into a crisp white button down and slacks, flinging over his arm a Tom Ford blazer I picked out for him. I open up my walk-in closet and survey the contents of my wardrobe. I pull out a white slinky Marc Jacobs sundress with small polka dots. It has pockets. Knee length white socks with blue ribbons. Comfy kitten heels. Mommy milf sartorial essentials. I put a Brandy crop top and Lululemon leggings into my bag for my Pilates class.

While the kids are still asleep, we make our way downstairs to the kitchen. I make him coffee before he goes to work. We sit out at our poolside as we sip.

Leaves float in the rippling blue water. A dead bee. For an LA summer, it's been unusually cold, and our swimming time has been relegated to beach weekends or sessions at the Equinox. The pool has been a little bit neglected.

"Darling, we really gotta hire someone to clean that."

"I'm on it. I'm on it today."

"You sure? I could ask around at work, see if anyone can give me a recommendation."

"Of course! You know I want to be proactive in the household."

"You got it."

"I could ask Mrs. Graham for her pool guy."

"We've had enough drama with the neighbors. Maybe you could find someone online, someone good and vetted."

"I'm sure I could just meet someone at the market."

"You never know who you'll find there," he laughs.

"Trust me baby, I'll crack the code." I wink at him.

"You always do. I love you, I'm off to work."

"I love you too, I'll let you know if I find anyone."

"Yeah, you just show them this dirty pool and sit back with a margarita. Let them do the legwork. But make sure it's good work."

We finish our coffees and I take our cups, rinsing them in the pink quartz kitchen sink.

"Do you find it hard to hire people?" I ask him.

"It depends," he considers. "To be honest, most people would not be up to par for the kind of roles I hire for. It takes someone special. Extraordinary. I scout for excellence."

"How do you know when someone's extraordinary?"

"I know you're extraordinary." He smiles. "You know it when you see it. When you know, you know. You just do. There's not a shred of doubt."

"Thank you, my love. And for your team? It must be hard to separate the wheat from the chaff when there's so many smart and talented candidates."

"Actually, I find it very simple. There's a woman whose research I've been reading. A Christina, something or the other. The stuff I've read of hers is unique, unlike anything else. I've been scouting her as a potential for our team. When an idea lingers in your mind, and you know it can not only turn a profit but be something that changes the world. Even if it's just your world, in the case of this pool for instance. Find someone you know will be a good fit. You'll know it when you see it."

An hour later the nanny arrives and the kids wake up. Who raising these damn kids??

While she rouses them awake, I make them breakfast. I've perfected my blueberry pancakes: fluffy, soft, souffle-like cakes with a little whip cream on top. Delightful. I take a bite to demonstrate its delightfulness to my kids.

"Mmmmm see how mommy eats these pancakes? Now you do that. Very good, DarkJulian. So proud of you, LaTesla. Okay now go with Ava and have fun today."

I pull them into a big hug. How soft their hair. How tiny their little hands, grasping at the hem of my white slinky Marc Jacobs dress.

"We'll be back at 7 o'clock, Mrs. Porcellian."
"Sounds good, see you then mwah."

12 hours of my own time on this day.

I'm off to the market. I'm off the market.

**A Crazy Ass White Boy Portal Has Opened**

After my weekly Pilates class at Cyan, I go into their sauna and take a shower at their studio. I scrub myself with their orange blossom body lotion. Oh, shit. I break a nail. I sit at the vanity mirror in their locker room fully naked, applying lotion and perfume all over my body. I bring the little travel size toiletries in my Galleria bag, their glass clinking like bells if I don't have any clothes to cushion them. Crispy mommy. I use their blow dryer on my hair, letting it set into long waves, while musing whether or not to just go home and relax, or be productive and do my beauty things. All the places I would ever need are at the market: gym, spa, shopping, food, coffee. I forget all about the quest line of the new employee.

Taking off my Lululemons and putting the Marc Jacobs back on, I decide fuck it. I want my nails. I want a facial. I want to feel like I've done something today. Time for some self-care. Time for some productivity.

I walk down to the Bellacures where Tracy glues on another spotless acrylic. I make an appointment at the Heyday for my monthly hydrofacial. I decide to grab a coffee at Blue Bottle, and just as I take that first sip and think once more about whether I want to proceed with more dailies, or leave and go home, someone approaches me from behind and calls my name.

I haven't heard his voice in almost two years, but I'd recognize it across all possible realities. Caleb. He was the love of my pussy but not the love of my life.

What if I'm hearing things? Suddenly I'm somehow sweaty with my dress clinging to my skin. Damn it I just took a shower. How inconvenient. I stop in my tracks in disbelief, not wanting to turn around. But I do. He says it again. "Colette?"

"Oh my god.. What are you doing on the west side?"

"I can't believe this.." he remarks.

"Wow." I raise my hand to tuck my hair behind my ear. My wedding ring flashes.

"You got married?"

"I did, two years ago. We have twins, a beautiful girl and a boy. I walked here, our house is just up the street from this market. I come here all the time."

"Wow. You got everything you wanted."

"Yes. I guess I did."

"What happened to the book you were writing? Cyber-horny? I never got to read it."

"Life's been so busy it got on the backburner, I shelved it for the time being. I might go back to it at some point, I don't know."

"I still want to read it."

"One day maybe you will, if it ever comes out. What's going on in your life?"

"I quit my job. I'm doing grad school at UCLA and just working on the side."

"Are you seeing anyone?"

"Uh, no, not right now.." he looks down.

I could tell I was starting to make him a little bit uncomfortable.

"Sorry, I don't mean to pry. I can't help but be a little curious." I giggle awkwardly. I change the subject. "So, you're here looking for work?"

"I was supposed to repair a painting for this guy in Santa Monica but he flaked on me today so I guess I'm just here wandering the market, grabbing a cold brew."

"Ah yes the cold brew, good to know you still like it."

"What are your plans for the day?"

"Just boring suburban stuff. Manicure, coffee, task of the day."

"What's the task of the day?"

I could've stopped myself there. Said 'nothing much, it was nice to see you', any variation of that, and moved on with my day. I could've walked away. But instead, I said,

"My task of the day is really to find someone to clean the pool. I'm actually looking for hired help, you know, as the woman of the house."

And I'm sure he could've stopped himself before he said, "Hello?" pointing his thumbs towards his chest, "Do you not remember me cleaning my aunt's fancy pool all summer? Joking about being the pool boy?"

"Oh yeah.."

Do I ever.

Several summers ago, we occupied the fancy pool at his aunt's house in the Hollywood hills. It was 80-something degrees out, and we were drinking beer in the afternoon. I stripped down to a tiny, strappy Honey Birdette snakeprint white bikini. The tan lines would be crazy with that one.

He cleaned the pool while I tanned, spread out on the poolside lounge chair serving, vaping, drinking. His cleaning was thorough, dedicated.

I walked in slowly from the shallow side, he dove into the deep end. We met in the middle. He picked me up and threw me around the pool. He kissed me and groped my body underneath the water. I could see a tan line forming already as he undid my top. It floated somewhere, off in the distance. My bottoms followed, floating through the pool like a pair of bedazzled jellyfish.

The pool scene in Showgirls comes to mind. I became horny, feral. I groped him back, discovering to no one's surprise he had a boner. I made eye contact while I kept my hand on his pants.

"I've never had sex in a pool before," I told him.
"Want to?"
"It's a sexy idea.. But I don't really like doing it in the water, it feels weird"
"We don't have to"
"I wanna do something" I said, adopting a serious and urgent tone as I continued to touch his throbbing boner. "We have to do something about this."

I led him to the shallow end of the pool where the entryway was on a gradual incline. I sat him down and took his shorts off, throwing them to wherever my own swimsuit was adrift. Fully naked, in the sun, in the shallow water, in heat, in love, in a slight drunkenness, I grabbed his hair and kissed him passionately, moving my kisses all the way down his body. I've never swallowed so fast in my life. After he finished, he said "wow, I owe you for that" and I floated in the pool face-up to the sky, letting it sizzle and cook me. My then-blue hair blended with the water.

Check me out. No tan lines.

I drift back into the present moment, momentarily distracted. He notices me disengaging.

"Hello?"
"Yeah, sorry yeah I remember that." I blush, which is uncharacteristic.

It's been a while since a guy that cute had flirted with me. And of course, with this particular cute guy, I'm uniquely placed with how to flirt back.

I become acutely aware of how my hair smells. Vanilla, cherry, peach in my blend of Tom Ford body oil, Carolina Herrera perfume, Versace hair mist. An undertone of amber in my L'occitane lotion. And underneath that, my skin. Sweating. It feels hotter than the 75 degrees my phone showed. Hotter than a demon in a sauna. The bar is in hell. The bar is in Satan's asshole.

"Your hair looks very pretty. I like the dark red on you." He says.
"Thank you. I haven't dyed it any weird colors in a while."
"Haha, did you outgrow that in your suburban life?"
"No, I just.. Only have the time for one color. The maintenance is insane between colors."

Seduction. It's an art best practiced on those who are vulnerable. Those who practice try to sway the susceptible, and when the seduction is successful, they ask themselves, was I seducing, or merely the one being seduced all along?

"Well, it looks great."

He bites his lip and scratches his hair. I remember biting that same lip and scratching my manicured hands through that same hair. I look him in the eyes and bite my lip, mirroring his sexy anxiety.

"So, did you want to see my pool?"
"Yeah, that'd be great."

He also, if for a moment, seems to have a flurry of distraction. I start to walk us in my house's direction, and wait a second for him to collect himself. He was a very anxious man. Girl, have you ever witnessed a male panic attack?

Kind of scary, kind of beautiful. His mental illness belonged to my old apartment for a long time. It was a part of me, even. Damn we both was psycho.

A crazy ass white boy portal has opened. Do I jump into this wormhole and let it careen me into an uncertain adventure, or do I stay put? Does he want to play games? Does he know I'm Jigsaw?

I remember, I start to teleport back to, the beginnings of our courtship.

Our romance began the old fashioned way – on a dating app. My best friend Britney had just gotten out of a long relationship, and turned to the unhinged dating app for some distraction.

"Come on," she tempted me, "it'll be fun, I don't wanna do this alone. You've been single for a while now, it's time to let loose."

I lazily downloaded the app and swiped, swiped, swiped. A lot of chaff on there. She was right, it was kind of entertaining observing these dudes with shitty pickup lines and overtly horny brazen nonsense. I got a good laugh out of it. Ok. Ooooh. He's kinda cute. What's all this then? I swiped right on a normal-seeming guy and we matched. On his profile, his prompt for what the best way to flirt with him was "be mean to me." I sent him a playful message: "fuck you bitch."

"haha. Investigate me, ms FBI" (I had FBI Special Agent on my profile)
"buy me a drink first"
"how about tonight?"
"sure"

Expecting a run of the mill date I'd probably walk out of not even through my first drink, probably no one who'd be a future husband, I decided anyway to meet up with him. I had indeed been single for almost a year since my last relationship. I usually date to marry, with intention for long term, but it would be nice to have a momentary glimmer of fun. At the very least, I'd have a story to tell my girls.

Fuck. We clicked instantly. I didn't expect this kind, sincere, handsome stranger, with whom I immediately felt familiar. It was just one of those all-encompassing connections: emotional, intellectual, physical. They say when you respond to pheromones, that's the body system indicating a perfect biological match.

"You don't actually work for the FBI do you?" he asked me.
"Nope." I laughed.
"So what do you do?"
"I'm a camgirl." I said frankly.
"Really?"
"Yeah I'm writing a thesis about my experiences in the online meat market. Here's the dissertation I have so far." I pull up a pdf on my phone of my concepts.
"Wow, cool. Ambitious lady."
"Not exactly. I'm quite traditional when it comes to a lot of things, like in relationships. This just happened to be a field I excelled in. I'm semi-retired now, and in my ideal life I'd be a trophy wife or homemaker. I'm different in my real life than in my work life. I don't date casually or do one night stands, I'm looking for a long term lifetime commitment someday."
"I'm a long term guy." He points to himself.

On one of our first dates, he asked me if I ever imagined my dream wedding. His sister was getting married soon, he said. I told him I'd always envisioned a ceremony that was iconic, but unpretentious. (And of course, a fabulous exquisite gown as frontispiece). Yes, I'd always dreamt of a romantic little wedding, no lavish or extravagant party, simply a party for close friends and family to celebrate a new union of love. He told me, "same." This gave me butterflies. This gave me hope. But as we all too well know, hope is a dangerous thing for a woman to have. Expectations are the gateway to disappointment.

With Caleb, when it was good, it was really good. The beginnings of new relationships always are. Those first few months, an oasis of newness, intrigue, intimacy, passion. He was my oasis in a drought. I thought I was undergoing a dry spell; he'd been single for six years before meeting me, so I certainly was his oasis as well. He told me he felt euphoric after our dates. He performed the role of suitor splendidly. He cooked dinner for me. He took me to the arcade and won me giant plushies. On our way back to my place from a sushi date, I'd kiss his neck and stroke his hair as he was driving. On the highway, I slipped my panties from under my dress, a thong embroidered with the phrase "passenger princess", and stuffed them in his mouth. Turning bright red, he sped all the way to my street and fucked me on the floor of my living room.

Euphoria. The sister of anxiety. We were both very anxious people. I suppose that connected us – in the realm of neurosis we understood each other. Our first sleepover in my bed, I couldn't sleep, tweeking into the night as I wondered what this all was. He talked with me until 4 in the morning and we spent a four day weekend together. By the end of that weekend, we were officially a couple.
That was some girlfriend-boyfriend psychosis. He was perving on my feelings.

I found myself developing strong feelings for him. Love

vibes. I just knew.

After my little bout of hysteria, I would then go on to witness a myriad of his panic attacks, bipolar diva meltdowns, and bourgeois crises. A true nepo baby, a spoiled LA rich boy, he could never quite connect the dots of how I did what I did because of the challenging cards life had dealt me. No I can't "just get a regular job" – because the work from home element of camming allowed me to take time off in a semi-retirement to have a personal life and date him, and arduous but lucrative sex work historically allowed me to take care of my disabled single mom. Yes, an unorthodox job for a woman who's trad at heart. Your redpilled problematic pornstar tradwife is crying. What are you gonna do about it? As they say, we contain multitudes. We are all a combination of despicable contradictions. Touch my boobs and repress my emotions.

"Dress for the job you want and you'll never work a day in your life," I quipped as I gave him a lap dance on my couch, tweeking my ass in his face, wearing nothing but Louboutin pumps.
"I never see you work."
"It's secretly boring and administrative. Besides, women shouldn't work. 24/7, 365,  I'm doing emotional labor."

I put my construction vest on and did emo boy heavy lifting. He was lucid, unlucid, grounded, ungrounded. I was bouncing off the walls clapping my booty cheeks.. I don't want to talk about it. No one teaches us emotional containing. Not all learning comes out of books.

Debriefing with myself one serene morning, I couldn't stop thinking about the intensity from the night before. After a dinner date in Ktown, and a weekend spent at his house in Echo Park, he was about to drop me off at home and go back to his. He cited a huge amount of work to catch up on at his dad's trendy gallery, where he worked as an art handler Monday through Friday. But right before I could gather my coat and purse, his tone shifted, his vibe turned solemn. I know a tweek when I see one. I remembered how in the restaurant, the tonal shift had already subtly begun when we made eye contact from across the table. The way he looked at me. I couldn't exactly identify that look, that gaze. I was fully intrigued and immersed, though, into his lovely stare, it was like dead serious but also soft and ethereal but not hollow. I don't know, indescribable. That and the anxiety attack, up down left right. We were in the trenches, the depths. I wanted to help alleviate any fear or discomfort he was having. That's what I was there for.

"Hey are you alright, do you want to come up?"
"No it's okay I have a lot of work to catch up on." He dismissed.
"Okay," I said, getting my keys. "But if you need anything, call me anytime."

I was just about to open the car door. We were in my garage driveway.
"Hey actually.." he panted, almost hyperventilating. "Can I come up? I'm having some anxiety."
"Oh my gosh, of course! Of course." I activated my garage gate controller. "I got you. You'll be fine."

We laid in my bed, where I held him. Tenderly, I stroked his hair and held him in my arms. We talked at length. His freakout was because, as he confessed, "I want to see you all the time. All I wanna do is hang out with you. I don't even have that much shit to do, whatever it can wait til this week, I just, I don't know what this feeling is but I want to be with you all the time."
"I do too. Those feelings can get intense and when the

relationship gets real, it's kind of scary. But it's also beautiful and magical."

"I lu.. l.. ugh.."

"Do you love me?"

"I'm in love with you, Colette."

"I love you too."

"Fuck."

"Does it feel good to say? It feels good for me."

"It feels so fucking good."

And he laughed.

After the cooldown in my bed, at last the declaration of love, the relief of finally having said it, we migrated to my living room couch and I brought us a cold Modelo to share. Just as I was about to hit my vape and turn on the TV to chill out, he suddenly and quite forecefully picked me up and carried me back to the bed, tossing me like a ragdoll and landing me on top of the memory foam mattress. He scaled my black thigh high stockings, reached under my red plaid skirt, and took my panties off, starting to vigorously go down on me. And I'm laying there shook in confusion, thinking, 'Omg what is going on are we gonna fuck for the 4th time this weekend? Sex IV: The Sequel?' It was unexpected, confusing, weird, hot, puzzling, baffling. I asked for my vape, and he brought it to me but continued. I lay there vaping while he ate me out. While part of me was shocked and frozen, a bigger part of me was turned on by this display of aggressive masculinity. Taking what he wanted. Devouring me. He looked me in the eyes, and then I recognized the weird look he gave me at the restaurant. It was love.

Love is terrifying. It's intoxicating. I was drawn to it like a moth to a flame, fluttering to my doom.

I do fear very well. I transmute fear and loathing into joy and sensuality. I alchemize tragic experiences into sexual experiences.

When I was hurting, I would imagine he was there with me. When he was hurting, he broke down. When we were both hurting, it was a disaster. The other parts of my life were contained, mitigated. Mostly, when I was hurting, it was about him. And when I was in my moments of crisis, he wasn't exactly receptive or comforting to me. He was, if anything, aloof and dismissive. Sitting on the couch pensively, "I don't know what else you want me to say."

I remember again, fast forwarding, this time something disturbing.

Tears streaming down my face, pathetically yowling a plaintive "I just want to be with someone who wants the same things with me as badly as I want them with you! Is me being a wife and a mom really that bad? Is the thought of me being your wife and mother of your children really so fucking horrible!?"

It had happened then, but this is now. This can't be real. This isn't happening. As we walk to my Brentwood home, his hand brushes up against mine. Of course I'm going to cheat on my husband with the pool boy. I'm so disgusted with myself. I'm also so turned on I can barely think straight.

The minute he enters my home to see the pool, I become even more nervous. My heart races. He looks around my house, observing its splendor.

"I'm shy."
"No you're not.. You're unbelievable."
"Careful, those are fragile." I tell him as he examines a

crystal vase.

"Is that.. cut crystal? It's exquisite."

"My husband has expensive taste."

"Clearly."

We walk on. I lead him outside.

"Well, this is the pool.." I twirl my hair and show him to the tool shed.

By this point he cleans the pool and I invite him in for a drink. While he cleans, I buzz around the kitchen. I start to kind of feel bad that he's out there washing the dead bees from the chlorinated poolblue water, and have the urge to invite him into the kitchen for a social call. I gather my cloves of garlic.

POOL BOY PASTA
1 delicious sexy fuckable pasta
1 extra slutty olive oil
2 cloves of garlic
3 sun dried tomatoes
4 basil leaves
¾ cup marriage-ruining marinara sauce

Mix ingredients into pan as you make pasta the way pasta is always made, but this time make a mess in your kitchen that can't be unmade. Burn the pasta, overcook it. So hot. ♡

"Hi," he crosses over from the yard, closing the glass screen door behind him. He's careful, quiet. He's good. Still, I'm startled. I turn around, almost freezing from fear.

"Hello.." I tap at the side of my wine glass. But when his eyes meet mine, and I really look at him, I understand. I am no longer afraid. He approaches me and I set my glass down. Fear turns into euphoria as the physiology of my body glitches.

"How long?" he asks.
"Long enough." I reply.

Without hesitation, he makes a move. His hands grab my neck, my hips, he kisses me hard. I kiss him back. I lean in, pressing my body close to his as he pushes me against the silver minimalist wall of my kitchen.

"God this is so wrong," I whisper.
"Then why does it feel so right?"
His hands roam over my dress, letting down its delicate spaghetti straps, pulling up its slinky skirt. I push his hands away with mine, feigning resistance. He takes the left strap and tears it, exposing my luscious fertile mommy breast. I gasp. I do nothing, I let him decide how he wants to do this.

"I'm all yours for another hour, make it count."
"I won't need that long."
"A quickie? You can't rush a work of art. As an artist.."
"You don't deserve an hour," he scolds. And I melt. This from the man who used to take his sweet time with undressing and worshiping every inch of my body, this sudden derogation activates some primal wiring for punishment.

He leans in to kiss me. Not on my mouth, no. On my neck. Then my chest. I grab his hair and wrap a leg around him, throwing off my heel. He picks me up and looks at me with an intense, savage gaze. Bending me over on the dining room table, he lifts up my dress and carelessly rips off my completely soaked pale blue Kiki de Montparnasse silk ruffle panties, stuffing them in my mouth. I arch my back to turn around and look at him. He pulls my hair.

The table shakes. He flips me around, and instead of continuing to fuck me right there on the table, he removes my gag and asks, "Where is your bedroom?"

"Upstairs," I answer breathlessly, "Second right."

With a swift motion he picks me up again and carries me up the stairs, down the hall, to the second right. He throws me onto the bed, puts a hand over my mouth, and fucks me like I'm his doll, his to use, his property. This side of him is so intoxicating that I haze out, losing much of my situational awareness. I'm in a weird, horny, dissociative headspace – it's like a drug. It comes and goes so quickly, and before I know it, we're back downstairs and I'm tidying up the kitchen, barefoot and naked under a paper cotton Anthropologie robe concealing my criminal body. I'm just about to reach for my fallen panties at the foot of the table when he picks them up.

"These are mine now."
"Okay," I comply, leading him to the hallway out. "I'll clean up here and be in touch about the pool."
"You can be in touch about anything," he delicately smooths my messed-up hair. "Don't vanish completely."
"I won't."

At the door, before he exits, he takes my face in his hands and kisses me – gently, tenderly, deliberately, deeply.

Once he leaves, I just sit still for a while. What a mess. The sheets are messy. The kitchen is messy. I'm sweating, my hair is greasy. I'm tired. His energy vampirism takes it out of me. But I need more. I don't know why, but I do. Maybe I'm addicted to suffering. This is the apotheosis of my girlhood.

Then the kids get home, dropped off by Miss Ava. I make them a snack in the same kitchen where I just got pounded senseless, and take it up to their rooms. I tuck them in, watch an episode of Booba Seals on iPad, and go back to the bedroom. Taking a deep breath, I trace my hands underneath my robe, lightly inspecting the mysterious bruises on my body. My husband won't be home for a while. I just want to sleep, but I keep looking at my phone. Waiting for some deus sex machina, a telepathic relay.

Be careful what you wish for. Right then, I receive a text from Caleb.

I write back, "♥"

"Tomorrow my place?"

"I'll be there. Addy?"

And so I do the opposite of vanish. I appear. I fucking reappear.

## Encounter: The Sequel

The next night I drive to Caleb's house in Echo Park, saying I'm going out with my girlfriends. This is wrong and it feels wrong, I know it will end badly but I can't help to.. Just.. Want.. One more night.

I put on a necklace that's been in my jewelry box for years, a delicate and dainty gold chain with a crystal deer charm, that Caleb had gifted me on our first and only anniversary. It looked striking next to the beautiful silver and diamond necklace my husband had gifted me on a trip to Hydra, our first trip abroad gallivanting in Greece, Albania, and Croatia. A visual manifestation of my duplicity, delicately choking my neck.

Parking in Echo Park was, is, always will be abysmal. I circle the block for 15 minutes, frustrated, and just call him.

"Hey I can't find parking I think I'm gonna drive home. I don't know."
"Let me park you."
"Ok valet boy."
He parks my car.
He stops.
He kisses me in the car.
The situation starts.

"You get something done?" he inspects my face.
"Bullhorn lip lift. Upper tooth show in repose. Blepharoplasty. Aligning my eye shape to optimize with my lateral thirds."
"You don't need any of that shit, you're beautiful without it."

His hand up my Dior dress.

Tracing my Agent Provocateur thigh highs.
Ripping my Agent Provocateur thigh highs.
Sliding his hand underneath my Bordelle thong.
I knew he knew how wet I'd be.
After all he's spent over a year perfecting how to make me
do this, and doing it to me over and over again.

"Wow.. you must really want this."

Slipping into my Bordelle thong with a middle finger.
Fuck you bitch.
Yes.. Fuck me bitch.
My YSL heels over his neck, falling off my ankles.
Taking off my Bordelle thong with his teeth.
Sliding his tongue inside me.
Tasting me like he's starving.. Devouring me.
I grab him by the collar and pull his mouth to mine.
I'm furiously unbuttoning his shirt.
Yanking it off with rage.
Scratching his back with my taloned nails.
He's biting my neck.
Taking off his pants.
Pounding me furiously.. Like he hates me.

★

I remember how furious he was with me when we broke
up. To be on the receiving end of a gentle, passive aggressive anger. The most toxic parts of me got.. activated.. when
he yelled at me. Lightly gaslit. Mildly manipulated. Called
me a gaslighter, twisted my words in a verbal litigation. We
have to negotiate this. We have to relitigate. He wouldn't
let me have the last word, he wouldn't let me leave, he
wouldn't let me win. He always had to be right. He always
had to win. It was so oddly masculine for him. I.. I.. I liked
it. Why? I'm diabolical.

"Hello?"

He says something as he slams my body in the backseat. I don't reply. I just continue heavy breathing. I'm not even sure I hear him clearly. When my eyes are open, they see nothing. I am no longer there. I think we finished.

Then he smacks my ass loudly and I am awakened back into reality.

"Oh I'm sorry, I must have.. I don't know." I shake my head.

"It's okay, it's okay, are you good?"

"Yes, very, oh I'm sorry please continue."

"Are you sure?"

"Absolutely." I nod.

He delicately strokes me and this time I am all at attention. Naked together, we just sit in the car, contemplating. I take out mommy's emergency vape from my little Prada bag and inhale a hit.

"Your husband.. why?"

"He promised to give me everything I ever wanted."

"And did he?"

"Yes."

"So why aren't you happy?"

"Why do you assume every housewife is unhappy? I love my husband."

"But you love me."

"Two things can exist at once.."

"Your mental gymnastics are insane."

"I can love you, and not love you, at the same time. I can love you, and not love you, and want to fuck you, at the same time."

"You don't not love me, though. You're here."

"Yes, perhaps you're right.." I sighed pensively.

In my deep, deep, deep confusion, I yearn to find a part of

me that's clear.

When I go home, I read Sylvia Plath. I'm awake for the first time in months. Psych ward of a gilded cage that is my trad wife trad life. I'm inspired to work on my book. Maybe the psychic was right. Maybe we do need feminism. Maybe..

I eat half a pint of Van Leeuwen honeycomb ice cream.
I listen to Bright Eyes and Lana Del Rey and nothing else.
I think about some things I haven't thought about in a long time, a cobweb in the attic of my mind decluttering and re-cluttering.

## Burden Sharing: A Gross Miscarriage of Justice

The bleakness of the 50/50 day.

If I struggle alone the same way as I struggled with these boys, what did I even need them for? Emotional support dusty. The duty of a man to be a provider and woman as nurturer has long since passed for many in this generation – which of course is advantageous to men. The one thing you should never do with money is use it as a weapon. But money is important. I don't have the luxury of being philosophically opposed to money. Unlike Caleb, who was from a privileged upper class family, I didn't grow up having it – I know how difficult it is to earn, survive, on my own as a woman. The desire for a provider to offer help goes beyond the mere numerical value of money. It's a love language, an integral and unignorable part of my love map. For a man to understand me as a woman, the suffering I endure every month, and to intrinsically want to lift that burden of agonizing fragileness. Two weeks out of the month I'm sufferingly physically or horomonally.. and the other two weeks, I'm suffering with him.

I am NOT a strong, independent woman by choice. There is no alternative. I always had to work for my living. I had no choice.

PTSD-like, it comes unannounced. Flashback.
"None of those motherfuckers are ever going to love you like I do."
"Do you even know HOW to love me?"
"Why is it all about money with you?"
"Yeah exactly – WHY is it about money, stability, security, have you ever wondered about the why?"
"When you're ready to cheat on your sugar daddy with the pool boy, you come knocking on my door."

"You want to be a cuck that bad?"

"Having a life premade for you is nothing compared to actually building a life with someone, with me, and you don't even wanna do the work, you say women shouldn't work in this outdated 1950s delusional view."

"No. It's not outdated, it's eternal. Women always want to be taken care of, and the way you make me feel crazy for wanting a family, wanting to be a stay at home mom, makes me feel incredibly hurt."

"There's no stay at home moms anymore! You should get another job if you need more money."

"But this isn't about money. This is not about a dollar amount. This is about values. This is about the mentality. If I was with a guy who I saw was grinding and working hard so that he could have a family with me one day and truly certainly wanted me to be his wife, wanted me to be his, I would naturally offer to help and ease his burden. Are you struggling financially?"

"No."

"We're not equal. We're not even financially equal. If you lost your job or your place, you have your family to help you. It's the opposite for me, if I drop the ball on my work I'm fucked."

"I know."

"So where's the equanimity there? Equality and equanimity are different things."


No one judges the woman from the looney bin when there's a stripper next door.


We've said things that stung, but for the most part we've tried to be logical and measured. We've been honest. We made an earnest attempt, it just didn't work.


"The way you bring things up is always so fucked up."

"You don't have that provider gene in you – never even

offer, hey Colette can I help you get your nails done? Are you ok on rent and bills this month? I want to help take care of you and make your life easier."

"Oh my goooooddd.." he rolled his eyes. "Don't you know? It's burden sharing. I'm carrying all the burdens of us being together: planning the dates, driving to you, driving you around, paying for the dates. You haven't paid for a single date."
"So it's a burden for you to spend time with me? It's a burden for you to do those things? As a woman, I'm not going to pay for any dates and I've told you this since day one. If you want 50/50 go date a dude or a masculine woman. If you want a feminine woman, you have to release her from her masculine burdens."

"Well.. it's not fair that I do things so much more than you do!"
"Not fair? That's how men are supposed to behave in courtship. That's what a man is supposed to do. You don't think I fucking work to be with you? You don't think I sacrifice? Really??"

"I'm putting in most of the work and you're just in the relationship."
"You view things your particular way, and I view things my particular way. They don't mesh, we've learned this. One way or another, sooner or later, it will be the end."

And I knew then – yeah, he's never going to propose.

The nerve of a guy to ask for 50/50.
No, I'm 5150.

But really – most guys will never understand the feminine psyche. How to be a good man, and take responsibility for their woman. How to claim her in the way she wants to be claimed.

"My clock is ticking, you don't understand shit."
"I do, I understand."
"No you don't!"

We had these fights, over and over again, cyclical and circuitous. They would resolve temporarily, but not really. Each micro-resolution was a band aid. The real wound, I was afraid, was not operable. There would have to be an amputation eventually, we were just prolonging it. In spite of this one thing, we did love each other. But again, sometimes love is not enough. And this thing, it was too big.
This wound, it was too deep.

The day before my childhood best friend's baby shower, I got my period. As if the blood in the toilet bowl wasn't enough of a reminder of my ticking fertility, I was having cramps of stomach-stabbing pain and a fatigue that felt inhumane, a wet blanket suffocating my body and mind. I was supposed to cook dinner for a few other friends that evening, but canceled last minute cause mentally, physically, I just couldn't do it. I had just completed a deadline at work, and it was a weekend to chill and socialize.

"Oh man.. sorry I'm so tired and gross today." I told Caleb as we were laying in my bed that afternoon.
"You're never gross."
"Thank you.. but ugh I can't with this fatigue. Just imagine how tired I would be if I had another job on top of this like you said I should. You think I never work, just because I work from home I don't do anything, but I work really hard."

"A little retail job isn't gonna be anywhere near as

exhausting as raising children. If you can't cook a dinner for a few people, how are you gonna cook dinner for your children?"

"You're right about some, this is what I think though – yes, kids are demanding, but it's a motivation and a pleasure to take care of them. Dinner for friends is different. I'd get up in the middle of the night to feed my kids and even though I'm tired it brings me so much joy. A low level job isn't just demanding, it's demotivating and weighs on the psyche. It's not something to take joy from, it's something that disheartens. Mothers do everything and more, 24/7, no breaks, no time off, because they are full of love and motivation. It's not an obligation."

Another wave of fatigue hits me. I lay on my side and I breathe. I feel myself bleeding. I feel myself hemorrhaging emotionally. Cue the snipers.

"Sorry I missed your baby shower, I was fighting with my boyfriend."

"Sorry I couldn't come to your brunch, I was up all night tweeking about my boyfriend and by the time the morning dawned I had a migraine."

"Sorry I couldn't make it to your wedding, I was afraid I would be too triggered because everyone there is married and I still feel single."

It was beginning to affect my social life.
If only the rest of our relationship was as compatible as we were in the bedroom.

"Burden sharing? Seriously, he calls it burden sharing?"
"Yeah as if I feel sooo daunted every time I drive to him or

sleep over or spend time with him, it's like the opposite it's something to look forward to."

I thought about ending it many times.

"Girl, just break up with him or cheat on him already, he's holding you back and as your friend I don't like seeing you like this." Britney tells me on the phone one day.

"Ughh. Fuck, I know. Believe me I tried. But every time I start to break up with him, I just can't do it. He pulls me back in. It's so fucking hard. I love him. I don't know what to do."
"No, girl, you know what to do. Be brave, you got this, we got you."

Was I a coward? A coward in love is the worst thing for a girl to be. There must be a special circle in Hell that Satan is engineering for me right now. Many people stay in relationships longer than they should, for various reasons. Some for convenience. Others, sunk cost fallacy. Others still, a delirious form of love. Nonsensical communication. Fatal attraction.

I tried to fix things. I tried, inauthentically to myself, to meet him in the middle. It just didn't come naturally to me. I can't fully go all the way, fully trust all the way, into a man who isn't certain that I'm his forever love. I wanted to give him commitment, eternity, fidelity, devotion. I wanted to give him forever. But because of this cyclical argument, I stopped myself.

This is not a man who would be a good husband for me. This is not a man who would be a good father for my children. This is not a man I'm meant to be with.

"I'm gender blind," he declared, "I don't see the difference between men and women."

Trad is alt now, and alt is the norm. In this progressive society, my traditional old-fashioned beliefs in relationships are considered unorthodox, a punchline, something I get made fun of. In a world of Feminist Fridays, I'm a Fertile Friday. One day I finally couldn't take it anymore and ended it. I wanted it to be civil and dramaless, with closure and gratitude and honor for the relationship's past, but with a history as lush, a connection as intense, it was painful.

"How did it go?" Britney checked in.
"I'm so sad." I bubble between tears.
"I'm so sorry, C."

It's over, it's really over, there is a pain that goes from my mouth to my chest. Pain is a part of girlhood. Wallowing in that pain. Taking mornings. Taking days. Stealing time. Doing time in the prison of my mind for stealing time. Time I enjoyed killing is never wasted. Hitting my vape in the morning, crying, smearing my mascara tears on my diary.

We had break up sex. One last time, I thought. The day after he left, looking at the mascara smears on my pillow from where he pounded me into it face first.

I asked him to serenade me once, on the little acoustic guitar that stood in my living room. He was a great musician. Play me a song darling. Sing to me. I've always desired that. He takes the guitar and starts playing scales, intellectual gooning on this little instrument. Not exactly a romantic serenade.

"Babe sing to me, please."
"I don't like my voice."

"Aww it's not about that. Some little chords and lyrics just for me?"
"No, I don't know, I just kind of like to noodle."
"I don't care how bad your voice is, it will always sound good to me."

"It wasn't even about him not liking his voice, it was about him like not showing up to learn my love languages, I feel like he didn't see me really, didn't hear me. And now I'm wallowing."
"Say more about that," the clinician said when I mentioned wallowing. I went back to my therapist after we parted ways.

"I find myself.. I don't know. Wallowing and just repeating on loop replaying our whole relationship, where it went wrong, trying to pinpoint the cracks, obsessing and ruminating."

"The repetition compulsion. Whatever you're doing, give yourself time, a set amount of time, to wallow. Put it into the grid of your day. Designate wallow time. You'll find it gets smaller and smaller as time goes on. Stop playing detective. It won't help you. Deeply thinking of the loss is a part of the grieving process, and therefore the healing process, but you need to shift eventually to actionable items, doing what's best for you, and moving on."

Was this part of the grieving process? The sudden insatiable horniness I felt? For a while before the breakup, I stopped feeling sexual towards Caleb – as my romantic feelings for him dissolved, so did my libido. But after we broke up, like a carnal ghost haunting my sex dreams, I couldn't stop thinking about fucking him. I didn't want to be with him anymore, I didn't need him. A huge emotional burden had been lifted. Physically, though, I was going crazy. I was in withdrawal.

I need your fingers inside me.
You're the only one I trust with your body on me, in me.
I need your red flags.
I need to be in the passenger seat of your car as you drive me home on the 101, taking my panties off and stuffing them in your mouth, almost causing an accident on the highway as you drive faster.
I need you in my bed, tweeking into the night.
But not really.

"It's so apparent to me that what we both want in life, in a relationship, isn't aligned and we will never be able to meet each other's needs. Sooner or later it will be over. If this continues, if we continue to be together, my feelings about uncertainty will get worse and you'll get frustrated and resentful with me and I never want to be the person who pressures you or makes you uncomfortable, so I think we should part ways." I told him through tears. "We shouldn't be together."

A long pause. My sniffles decorated the silence.

"Damn." He said finally. "I knew it. I saw this coming. This sucks."

"I know. I hate that it's come to this, my heart is already so broken and I love you so much but it's not fair to either of us to be together anymore."

"It's hard to hear."
"I know it's hard to hear. It's hard to say."

He suppresses it, but I can hear his eyes welling up. A faint sniffle to echo mine.

"I love you and I want you to be happy and get what you want. It makes me feel like shit that I can't give you what you want. I feel embarrassed, I feel all the negative emotions towards myself for trying too hard at this thing."

"I'm thankful for everything though. I have no regrets."
"You're a really smart woman, Colette. Don't sell yourself short."
"I never do."
"Bye."
"Bye."

And that was all. And then he was gone.

'Get what you want' huh.. painting me as selfish, self serving, inconsiderate, greedy. Embarrassed for trying too hard.. I was never embarrassed to try hard. It's as though I wasn't giving it my all and I wasn't putting any effort into this thing. He did think that way though. That I allegedly wasn't doing my part of the fucking burden sharing.

Boy was you wrong.
I prioritized him. I gave him my time, my body, my soul, my energy. It's different for women. But he thought men and women were the same, were no different. Every time I have a glimpse of missing him, I remind myself of this. I could miss his body, I could miss his presence, but I'd never miss his mind.

The repetition compulsion made its way into my diary as I scribbled out nonsensical scrawlings on mascara tear stained pages. Letters I would never send, because what I wrote, I've said it all before. According to my therapist, the repetition compulsion exemplifies that we as humans have a soul, a flawed imperfect soul that makes us human and not automaton.

I'm fucking done!!!!!!!!!

All this time of knowing me, and I don't feel like you get me.

'Get out there babe, put yourself out there, be independent, go out and do your thing, you got yourself' – as if I haven't. I have never not been independent and I have way too much agency. I want a man who will cage me. Contain me. Lead me.

I'm tired – not from my job, but from life and all the beatings I've taken in being too independent and assertive.

Every single fucking day I wish I had some kind of security beyond only relying on myself – and saying things to me like you got it, put yourself out there, work more – as if I haven't already been doing that – feels hurtful and ignorant.

Why do I even need a relationship if I struggle just as much as I do alone?
Comparing men to women.. ridiculous.

Exit wounds.
When your reality is shattered and you're mourning a future.
It's like we were both addicted to each others drama and enough was enough.
Oh prince shall my kisses break the silence.

It's like surgery – you know you need it and you know it's going to hurt.
Girlhood and pain on writer Wednesday.
Girlhood rage.
It's too late.
Girl pain.

You're the only one who I've craved sexually.. but does it make you a good husband? No.

Do you know why I really saw a future with you? You're kind and you're sincere. It's a rare quality in this city.

Married life means making it work!! I guess we couldn't! Divorce!!!

Getting through hell together, getting through each other's hells.

Ironed pillowcases.

To be a porn category.


He systematically pulled me apart, piece by piece, until there was nothing left but pain. Towards the end.. when I knew it was coming, when we both knew. Why were we holding on when we knew it wouldn't work? Because love. Because that cocktail of neurons and chemicals, that raw primal visceral connection that comes once in a lifetime if you're lucky. That unexplainable, intangible magnetic pull you feel right away. From the first moment.


Take me back to that first night, I pleaded with the universe. I want to go back. I want to stay there, in that night, in that moment, forever. But life doesn't work that way. Eventually, the cracks begin to show. Even in the most chemical of romances.


I could feel the tension of him withdrawing, even over a text. Even distances away, I could feel the energetic cord of his anger penetrating my psyche. To counter this strike of anger, I apply my own pain to this energetic cord. Yes, I learn from the very best, how to play the victim card. A high stakes game of emotional poker. From the most delicate of males, I learn over time how to become the very best female manipulator I can be. I'm selfish, greedy. My outfit costs 3500 dollars but being in an abusive relationship with me is free.

Stop. I have to stop right there. Being an abuser is masculine energy, and being NOT abusive is being in my feminine. I'm sincere, earnest. Too vulnerable for my own good. Vulnerable for my own bad. My silk sheets and soft comforter cost 3700 dollars but being wrapped up in my soft gentle embrace is free.

The day I broke up with him, I entered into a new relationship with my anger. With my sadness. With my misery. Still, I saved a special place in the dungeon of my heart for him. What was once love had soured, and is off to the dungeon to be devoured. And reborn, as illumination. A new blessing to come. It's not over, it's just beginning. The life that has always been meant for me.

The beauty of fertility, after all. My children were born on June 14th, a natural birth for Gemini twins. It was the most difficult, beautiful, intense moment of my life. The doctors at Cedars Sinai were incredible. God bless the epidural. It's ok honey mommy can vape while pregnant.. Pregnant women switch to beer.

"None of those motherfuckers are ever going to love you like I love you." It echoes in my head like a sonic weapon. This frightens me.

Caleb was wrong. My husband loves me very much. Softly. Daringly. Frequently. Well. Less frequently now that we've had kids, but he does love me, I can feel it. It's a different kind of love, though. I love him too. I love being a possession. I love having security and stability. I love how he loves me. He sees me. He really listens. He loves how I love him. We understand each other on a deeper level than goonfest discussions of intellectual drivel, or sparks-flying feral carnality. We have a home together, kids, a life we both put in effort to build.

**Trophy Wife**

Luckily, I wasn't the starter wife. His ex-wife was a ball busting businesswoman he'd met when he was first starting out in the tech industry. She'd flown circles around him, sharked every promotion imaginable, finessed a top position at a software company. He was attracted to her for her ambition and intelligence, but filed for divorce when their home life was all work and no play. Work is already all work and no play, but the home life – it needed a softer approach.

That's where I came in. No grand career ambitions, just an ambient love of fashion and a goalless praxis of writing. I loved clothes. I loved books. I loved love. Romance. The intoxication of desire. My husband found it refreshing, feminine, alluring. We balanced each other out, our energies supporting one another.

I saw a psychic once and I remember her telling me: "you're a writer – so write".
"I don't know what to write."
"Write what you know."

The cyclical zen. Was that supposed to inspire me?

I haven't been feeling very creatively inspired recently. Life was too good. I had no pain. I had no muse. But behold, he came back into my life one day and became my muse. He gave me pain. But pain was not enough. Pain was too much. Pain felt like nothing; am I anesthetized?

When I think of my husband, I have no magnetic chemical sparks, I tweek none. I feel a calm, like he is my rock, my container. I feel a peaceful gratitude.

You hear of this often – the union of convenience, the

passionless marriage. He's busy. He gets busier and busier. I'm more and more alone. But the quotidian mundanity – I love it. I don't mind the alone time; in fact, it helps our marriage thrive. It's a blessing. It's stability. It's security. It's something I've never had.

I met my husband on a dating website for wealthy men looking for beautiful women. He gave me an allowance for the times we'd meet, and it progressed into a relationship, then a formal commitment, then a marriage. He bought a house in Brentwood for us to live in. Close enough for my mom to visit, far enough for her to not get on my nerves. I talk shit but she's amazing with her grandchildren. She wanted a car, so we bought her a car. A beautiful white Tesla Model Y (not related to my daughter LaTesla.)

Our arrangement might sound clinical, but it worked for us. Still, I looked for something to fall in love with other than his fuck-you money and the promise of security and certainty. His smile melted my heart, every time he'd laugh at my inappropriate jokes. We shared a dark sense of humor.

"What's your favorite quote about relationships?" I asked him on our second date.
"Sharing a bed with a woman is like sharing a bed with the CIA."
"Wait, you're a Gaspar Noe fan?"
"Oh yeah, Love and Enter the Void are some of my favorite films."
"That's so unexpected!"
"Well, one day when we're sharing a bed together we'll probably never run out of trippy movies to watch."
"Do you like David Lynch?"
"I do." He held my hand and brushed his lips against it. His gaze went soft, and I had a sudden urge to kiss him. I gave in to the moment when he kissed me.

Kissing is like time travel. We time travel with our kisses, and with our thoughts. The mere thought of a simple kiss can take me back more than the thought of just straight up sex. Maybe I am a hopeless romantic at heart.

And when the time came when I had thoughts, a desperate anxiety that couldn't be contained, he would hear me out, no matter how unhinged and retarded.

On a full moon by the waters of the Pacific Ocean as he took me out on his boat in Marina Del Rey, he asked me to marry him.

"Is that all I will become in life? A bored, lonely, horny housewife?"
"I've always wanted one of those."
"You know what, me too. I've always wanted to be that."
"Well, be mine. Say yes."
"Yes!"

My heart pounded as he put the ring on my finger.
A delicate rose gold band with a princess-cut pink diamond.
It was flawless.

The wedding was iconic and unpretentious, with only close friends and family attending. I wore a spectacular, timeless custom Marchesa. On our wedding night, in the penthouse suite of the Beverly Hills Hotel, I stepped out of the boudoir in nothing but gold body jewelry and my curves adorned in sheer silk scarves. I cued a classical playlist and slinked towards him with a slow sultry dance.

"Hello dear. How do I look as your wedded wife?"
"Extraordinary, so moving, so sensual. I love you."
"I love you, Mr."

I gave him a lap dance to the Tchaikovsky Arabian Suite. Sat him on the gold velvet chair, tossed white rose petals all around us. Straddling him with my legs, I bent backwards and articulated my spine back up, kissing the side of his neck. All that ballet training had to go somewhere. I wanted to give him magic he will never forget.

Rose petals on the floor.
Rose petals on the bed.
Rose petals in the champagne glass.
Rose petals in the bath as I decompressed and smiled to myself.

Oh, my husband, my dear, my darling, my beloved. I want to have intimacy with you. Even if just holding your hand before you fall asleep. The wisdom you provide, having lived longer than I, having such attractive ambition which allows us this privileged kind of life.

I don't need wild sex in a basement, blow jobs in the pool, Showgirls-esque displays of sexual acrobatics. The stability, the safety – that IS sex to me.

"This is for you."
That night he gifted me a chain of gold, diamonds and pearls, more beautiful and extravagant than anything I've ever had the delight of wearing. When I laid down next to him in bed, I wore only that.

Marilyn Monroe once said the only thing she wears to bed is Chanel No5, or just diamonds. I felt Marylin in the room with us right then.

Without a symbol, what is a story? It's just masturbatory thinking. Verbal gooning.

For our honeymoon, he took me to Italy. It was the best two weeks of my life. As we made love on the terrace of a Tuscan villa, sipped Aperol Spritzes by the Colosseum, rode a gondola in Venice, I sighed, "what have I done to deserve this? How did I get so lucky?"

"Hey. You're mine. You deserve the world. And I want to give it to you."
"I think my ice cold heart just melted."
"You mean this warm, soft heart of melted gold?"
As he stroked, gently squeezed my chest. This luscious bosom which underneath contains a beating heart, a racing pulse, a horde of subjectivity.
"I think I've been waiting my entire life to have someone say that to me and really mean it."
"Those guys who didn't want to give you the world.. they should be in a straightjacket."

I should be in a straightjacket.. I thought. Sectioned. 5150'd. So I got the life I wanted. The perfect, premade life, the magnificent gilded cage. At what cost?

Why would I disrupt a life this perfect? What have I done? I only think after I do. I'm afraid, I'm horny, I'm bored, I'm unraveling. Laying in bed after a night with Caleb, I'm unraveling. And still, I keep being drawn to more nights with him. I relentlessly tell myself my affair will be short lived. That he will live on in my imagination and memory.

And in my dreams. I keep waking up after having lascivious dreams about Caleb. In one, he brings me flowers beyond belief. In another, he's on top of me and I can't escape. A sexy sleep paralysis. Torrid caresses, soft kisses, passionate cries of ecstasy. The only thing missing from these dreams is my husband, who comments on my yowls when we awaken in the morning. I flush in shame.

"Was I talking?"
"More like moaning."
"We can recreate it once we end our drought."
"It was pretty kinky stuff.." I admitted.

I feel like myself again, all things considered.
Feeling fertile.

How is the person I sleep next to at night betraying me?
Can you forget?

Encountering Caleb at the market, that fateful day..
Then again at my house..
Then again in my car..
Then again at his house..
Again and again, in a blur, those few days gooned..
Until I tell him his short-lived services as a pool boy will no
longer be needed as the summer is coming to an end.
My necklaces get tangled. I take it as a sign.

**The Return**

As I drive home from the final whirlwind evening on the east side, reapplying my lipstick on the red light on Sunset and La Cienega and putting my hair back in place on the stop sign at Burlington and Hanover, I reflect on the crucible of the past week. The prodigal slut returning home to her loving family from a spicy reunion with ex boyfriend. Returning home. Home. What a beautiful, elusive, difficult word. With my husband, my children, the fairy tale, I finally belonged.

But did I? Flashbacks violate me against my will. Fighting them off, I park a block away from home to give myself a moment to mentally debrief before I port into our picturesque rose-adorned driveway.

A spindle, a darkness, a fever, a necklace.

The two chains wrapped around my neck wind around one another, chaotically entangling a wraith of silver and gold that has begun to destabilize me. I fumble despite my talon manicure to remove the silver chain. Goodbye, crystal deer. I pull into the driveway, neck clean and absolved with pure gold, the diamonds sparkling beneath moonlight as I turn the key in the glittering knob that heralds the entrance to home.

"Honey I'm home!" I call out from the foyer.
"Heyyy darlin! Where've you been?" He calls from the upstairs bedroom. For once, he was home early.
As he walks down the stairs I feel a massive sigh of relief, and as he wraps me in his arms I feel a joy wrapping my body.
"Oh honey.. I've been on my bullshit."
"Enough of that. Come kiss the kids good night."

I walk up the stairs, down the hall, to the children's room. It looks like what I imagined my room would look like when I was a child. Blue and lavender pastel wall paint, giant collections of stuffed animals, colored pens scrawling onto the ripped pages of blank-sheet art diaries, rudimentary tech toys for learning how to be smart. Their bedding is cloud patterned, they sleep in their beds so peacefully. I no longer have that pastel princess maximalism, I no longer have that peaceful night of sleep. But I have them. I cuddle DarkJulian and LaTesla.

"Now come kiss me good night."

That night I kiss my husband passionately, inspired more than ever from the electricity of my encounters. In bed, he traces my body with his fingertips, bites my neck and whispers in my ear how he can't wait to make up for lost time by ravaging me senseless after he comes back from this weekend's business trip. How he'll take me out to Arva, take me for a spa day at Ole Henrickson and a shopping trip at Neiman, and take the next week off to do nothing but worship me.

Yes, there was a reason I married him. It wasn't just the money. It wasn't just the mansion, the ring, the children. The material luxuries, god they are nice, but it was just the cherry on top of the creamy sundae of a mutually shared life. It was his vision, uniting with mine. It was the promise. He kept me safe. He gave me security. He had the provider gene, and I was the lucky lady he chose to love.

Love is a choice. It's an action. Every single day, we choose to love. It happens. The messes we make. When you make a mess, you have to clean it up. When you make a mess, you have to suffer the consequences.

I remembered one of my last fights with Caleb. How I shared my thoughts, and how he dismissed them. How I picked an inopportune time, an angsty tone. My hysteria so high he couldn't even scale it. Fine, I'll never bring this up again – I'll shut the fuck up. A meth lab exploded in my heart.

I can take my thoughts and put them in a box and put a lid on it, but eventually there will be so many thoughts even a lid can't hold them and I'll spill out a mess.

Ah, yes. The stenographer of memory writes injustices in bold. The warden of adultery casts prisoners into a rose garden watered by snake venom.

Flower-like years.
I lay in interrogation with myself.
Pillar of salt.

"Hinge nevermore. We've seen what's on Hinge.. nothing good on there. It's all cripples, fuckboys, and nepo babies."
I remember how Britney said this to me after my breakup.

I have a dream the neighbor chick realizes about the affair and makes me share the new pool boy.

I have a dream that there are two Calebs and I have a threesome with them.

I have a dream I live alone in a three bedroom apartment and Caleb is the mailman who delivers the presents my gentlemen callers send me. Mailman. Male man.

"Two men for each of us, and we don't know what the hell to do with any of them," Norma Jennings said to Shelly Johnson at the Double R Diner in Twin Peaks. Is that me now? Two men in my life, and a whirl of emotional gymnastics? A collection of contradictions. But I untangled the necklaces, I cleaned the mess. I reconciled the contradictions. I made my choice.

Compassion and cruelty can live side by side in one heart, and anyone is capable of anything.

I'm just crazy. You can put me into my dream life and I'll still be crazy.

Whistle a tune, as I'm digging a grave on a hot afternoon. The next day I wake up and clean the pool myself. I call my good judy.

"Britney, what am I going to do?"
"It gets messy, girl. Follow your heart. You know exactly what to do. It's time to be brave."

Pain is beauty, and I am the prettiest.

I clean the pool in a baby pink sequined Selkie gown, one of many in my closet. It trails behind my feet, almost touching the grime I pull aside with the pool net.

Caleb always thought those dresses were too much. He despised the thought of buying me a dress. His gifts to me were mostly practical: kitchen knives, stove pans, oven thermometer. I appreciated that those, comically, aided me in becoming the domestic goddess I am now. I dip a toe into the clean pool, the wind blowing a piece of my frivolous skirt into the water. It's so delicate and impractical, but fashion is not meant to be practical. It's made this life such a joy to live.

TRAD WIFE WAFFLES

DRY ingredients: mix them together – flour, sugar, baking powder, baking soda, salt
WET ingredients: mix them together – (make your own) buttermilk, melted butter, large eggs, vanilla extract

Whisk the DRY and WET ingredients in a bowl, be sure not to over mix. COOK in a heated-up waffle iron: pour about ½ - ⅓ of the batter into the iron and top with syrup, berries, or any other topping you may desire! ♡

**The Consequences**

Two weeks later, I get out of bed and feel a tangle in my stomach, a wave of nausea that makes me throw off my robe and hurtle to the bathroom. Holding on to the marble counter, I lift up the black porcelain toilet lid and open my mouth. I try to suppress it, but it spills out. Weakly, shakily, I collect myself and rise back up. What the fuck. Was it the shrimp linguine from Avra? I hadn't had any cocktails or alcohol. As soon as I get up, I feel a little better. Maybe I should eat something. Putting my robe back on, I walk downstairs to the kitchen.

It's 6:12AM on Toilet Bowl Monday. The kids are asleep and my husband is already at work. I rub my belly. Bread smells weird to me. Butter, even worse. I rack the fridge: there's a honey chevre goat cheese that I usually can't stand, that makes my mouth water all of a sudden. Cheese cheese cheese. I dig in. Greedy, lustful, possessed by something inside me that isn't me, I eat two servings.
The cheese speaks to me.

I get in my Tesla and drive to the walgreens. My heart is pounding, its ass cheeks clapping on my aortal chamber door.
The one time in my life I wish to make time speed up.
A quickie? It takes time to create a work of art. As an artist. As a time lord.

In the end..
I take the damn pregnancy test. I haven't had sex with my husband in months. The test comes out positive.

I inhale another slice of cheese. I take another deep breath. Now I eat and breathe for two. There it was. The double blue line. Proof of life.

*My desire and my dignity — I pushed them to
opposite ends of the room.*

*There's nothing to do but nothing.
There's nothing to do but everything.*

*Catch
the
heart
off
guard
and
blow
it
open.*

**$CMPT**

Always busy. I'm always busy. Making money. Splitting hairs.

"Babe come back to bed," Conor calls from the bedroom room. A door away, I'm in the bathroom tweeking into the night, hunched over the white quartz counter, putting the finishing touches on the Lattice embedded in my palm. After my evening shower, I'm beautiful and clean. Hair soft and pastel pink. Face exfoliated. 95.5 lbs soaking wet. Pure, except for my left hand. I exhale at myself in the LED lit mirror. With my right hand, I perform surgery on my left.

The Lattice is a biotech device I developed, meant to be fully integrated with my palm. Its thin geometric pattern slices into my palm, drawing blood that spills in a few drops on the countertop. Extending from the palm interface, a thin wire wraps around my wrist and penetrates my forearm like an IV. Once set, it will use the natural electricity from my body to activate. Its function transmutes –

"Babe!"
"One sec!"

I hastily crack open the mirrored cabinet, take out some gauze pads, and pat pat pat all over my left arm. Quickly, the blood flow subsides and the Lattice lights up. It finally lights up. Omg. I run into the bedroom to show Conor my creation.

"It's activating!"
"What is?" he asks, cozied up in bed with a blanket half-

folded over him, one hand on his tablet and the other behind his back on the quilted headboard. I dive in bed next to him and tunnel my way under the other half of the blanket.

"My desire for you," I say playfully, touching his face with my lit palm.

"So is this the thing you were working on?"
"Oh my god, babe yes! My Lattice – my device, my patent, my baby."

I unfold my hand onto his lap and he examines it.

"Very cool, congratulations! I'm proud of you."
"Thank you."
"What about a baby of our own?"

I freeze. Hell, I just gave birth. The umbilical cord is still in. My baby, the Lattice, is still weaned onto mother's teat. Quick, think. I shift my mind and think sexually. Breeding kink. Okay, this I can work with.

"Oh yeah, you're gonna cum in my little mommy pussy and make me a dirty little milf, huh?"

I trace my hand down his chest down his torso and straddle him. I undo the tie of my silk robe, slipping it off my body, and guide his hands to remove the straps of my lace neg-ligee. I look at my hand and it glows a pale pink, pinking harder and brighter with more arousal.

"My fertile window is open."
"That's so hot."

"Tell me I'm a sexy little mommy and you wanna knock me up."

"You're a sexy little mommy and I wanna knock you up."
"You're gonna cum inside me raw tonight."
"I'm gonna cum inside you raw."

It must be noted he has never actually finished in me. Me, I was afraid of him not pulling out. He, wanted full enthusiastic consent before doing something like that. His pull out game was remarkable.

Sex is of course reproductive, but there's a thousand other ways to be a mommy so I viewed sex as recreational.

"Yeah, that's right. Your dirty little mommy, I'm ovulating and fertile." I purrrrred. But then the vibe shifted. Contorting myself into this false fantasy of a fertile female, I felt him go limp. This was a first.

"I don't know, this isn't working for me." He said, gently lifting me off him and back onto my side of the bed.

"I'm sorry," I whisper. "What's wrong?"
"If you were really ovulating and fertile.. you.. it's like a game to you but I really want this. The fantasy isn't enough anymore. You really don't want to be a mommy? With a baby of our own?"

I pause and sigh. Look him in the eyes confused. We've had many fights about this recently, but this is the first one that ever stopped our having sex.

"Babe.. I.. I don't know."
"You don't know?"
"I don't know what to say."
"How about a yes?"
"Well,  I don't know,   maybe, one day.."
"That doesn't sound very enthusiastic."

"Well I don't want to lie to you or spout empty platitudes."
"You mean to say you've never thought about it? Me and you? Our future?"
"Honestly I haven't really thought that far ahead."
"So as a woman you've never imagined your future self, like, getting married or having children?"
"I guess it just wasn't that big a part of my headspace."

I pause pensively and take his hands in mine, moving my own hands up his arms and cradling his face.

"You know I love you, right? I love you so much."
"I know. I love you too. I'm sorry to bring all this heavy shit up."
"It's okay. We can talk about anything. I just want you to know I love you so much and we're here together now and we'll have so many more beautiful adventures and it's beautiful."
"I love you so much too."
"We have a lifetime ahead of us. We'll get there, baby."
"Okay."
"Okay? Let's not go to bed angry. It's already so late. I can't have another sleepless night with us arguing about this. Please. I only have love for you."
"Good night baby."
"Good night," I kiss him on the lips. "Oh, and hey, I'll make it up to you."

I fall into my pillow.

Sleep cues. I begin to think about sleep, and imagine myself in a deep calm, waves of calm undulating over me as I fade into the night. The Lattice glows blue. Pretty soon, I pass out.

The next morning I wake up to my new prototype alarm.

The first thing I see when I wake up is my hand glowing red. Good morning. I feel an influx of energy as I fully open my eyes. I haven't coded much into it yet, just some basic smartfunctions like alarm, reminders, and sleep cues.

I must prepare for a keynote speech today. Yesterday's speech went very well, and I have another lined up for to-night. My new product, the Lattice, which has been acquired by Porcellian Industries, will change the game of artificial intelligence.

I have a meeting with Dr. Porcellian himself. For a second, when I first met him, I thought he was hitting on me when he gave me a wink after one of my closing remarks.. but who am I to delude myself when he works 100 hours a week and has a loving wife and beautiful children. There is simply no time to have extramarital affairs. They have produced heirs. What the hell have I been doing with my life?

This. Working almost as many hours as the doctor, developing line after line of code that creates archetypes of personality and consciousness. If I can pull this off, we'll have successfully solved the problem of subjectivity. Our programmed tulpas can have personality traits based on real people, and those personality programs could be wired into a human brain to instantly develop or enhance a characteristic. The Lattice relates to this as it would be the medium by which the personality characteristics are encoded and transferred.

```
>|{ lattice synthesis #include <<x skill>>
[tmp1; DNA pushback {none}]
| mscl atrophy = heal; }
```

Green for go. Orange for no.
Bitcoin is up this week. Profit margins extremely high.

I'm a pretty girl. And pretty girls are never lonely. But even in a relationship, I can still feel so alone. Conor recently started asking me when I'm going to want to get married or when we'll have a baby. These conversations have been increasing in frequency. Even if I have the latitude to focus on that right now, I just don't want to. The desire to mother, in me, has always been drawn to the inanimate. My lines of code are my children. My bitcoin wallet is my womb. The stock exchange is my sperm donor.

Looking at my glowing red hand, focusing my eyes after my mind, I look at the other side of the bed and notice Conor isn't there. Strange. He usually sleeps later than I do. I hear some hustling and bustling in the living room so I get my ass out of bed and investigate. I slip my robe off, leave it on the bed. In my see through lace negligee, I walk out of the bedroom to see him working on his laptop in his boxer shorts.

"Hey sexy." I shake my ass, trying to get his attention. I start to shimmy my dress off, teasing him seductively.
"Oh hey sexy." He doesn't look up.
"You're up early."
"Yeah, I didn't sleep that well, my brain was kind of activated all night."
"Ohh I'm sorry, what are you thinking about?"
"Just some last minute work stuff I have to catch up on."
"Oh okay."

I go into the bathroom and brush my teeth. I wash my face. I brush my hair. I step on the scale – 94.9 lbs naked and dry. A personal best. In my little achievement oriented disorder, I magically get a little bit lighter each time my research soars. The fatter the wallet, the thinner the waist. I know, I know. Not a great coping mechanism, but let me worry about that later. Even thinking about how my body will change if pregnant .. makes .. me.. sick.

I take my cute little yoga mat out of my storage and lay it down in the living room, doing stretches in the nude. Conor still doesn't look up.

As we do our morning routines, and I go to kiss him, I notice he doesn't kiss me back like he always does. I try to slip him the tongue. He is cold and stiff, almost pulling away.
"What's wrong? Am I gross today?" I ask.
"No you're not. It's nothing, I don't know, I feel weird, but it's maybe nothing." Conor averts my gaze as he pours coffee from the fridge for the both of us.
"Well it's not nothing if you feel weird," I question him, taking my glass and sipping.
"It's.. ugh. It's what it always is," he sighs exasperatedly. "I find myself stuck in my head about your uncertainty if you want to be a wife and a mother or not. I see everyone around me starting a family with their loved ones and I want that. We're at that age, you know."
"I know."

I sip my coffee slowly, trying to measure my quickening breathing and racing thoughts, but it becomes difficult to focus. I sense my heartbeat interacting with the biotech geometry in my palm, and I rattle in my chair as he sits down opposite me at the table. You can cut with a knife the tension in my apartment's dining area.

"Is it about that baby thing yesterday?" I gently trace my Lattice.
"Yeah."
"Look, we both have work soon, can we revisit this at a different time? We're both stressed out and on edge, let's just circle back, ok?"
"Hey, you said to talk about it."

"I know, but this is, actually, a bad time. You need to get better about your timing, because when it's presented to me like this, I get frustrated."

"And I get frustrated when every time I try to bring up our future, you recoil."

"I know I'm selfish, unhinged, and ambitious," I warn him. "I have to get a little bit further in life before I can make a decision like this. Before we can make a decision this big, together."

"Yeah, that's fair, but I just I don't know, I need some form of reassurance and certainty in the now."

"I can't give you that certainty," I explain to him, "I'm married to my job. My patent is my baby. I love you, but I'm on the edge of something visionary and groundbreaking – I have no time, I'm too busy to settle down like this."

There's a silence. I mentally calculate how long it will take me to get to work. The minutes shorten as time stretches, dilates, in this awkward silence.

"Doesn't the idea of a family with me excite you?"

"I've never 100% wanted children, you know that. I have my reservations."

"You're breaking my heart. I'm standing in front of you with this vulnerable headspace and it feels like you don't care."

"Of course I love you and I care about you but.. It's my body. My body on the line."

"Christina, please–"

"Conor, I can't do this right now. Later, please."

"Ok. But come on, Steve Job-ess. You know I'll take care of you. I'll take care of our family."

"I don't need you to take care of me. I like our life now. I like my life now, being independent. I want an equal partnership, like we have now.. I love our dynamic."

"I want to be with a woman who can give me a certain

answer because I deserve that. It's like a bell, you can't un-ring it, alright?"

He locks on to me with an angered vision. I do what I can to calm it, to give him even a shred of reassurance.

"Yes.. you're right." I get out of my chair and walk over to give him a hug and a kiss. While it's small in the grand scheme of things, it's massive now. He sighs and puts his arms around me. We breathe. We say nothing.

We take a pause. Resolved, but unresolved. A stalemate. We both have work in less than an hour. I gather my laptop and today's outfit, and he goes to take a shower.

While he is in the shower, his phone rings and gets several alerts. The device is right next to me on the bed, I look over – I figure I'll tell him if his friends or family called or something, the way we normally relay things to each other. I don't recognize the name that is contacting him. It's a woman. Oh god am I really doing this? Against my morals, on autopilot, I'm violating the terms of his privacy policy and looking at the messages on his phone. I can't even process what they say. I just see this pretty, feminine lady. He's looking for a way out.

I literally don't have time for this, I have to go to work. (Compartmentalizing ($CMPT))

"Alright I've gotta get out of here. I'm late for my lobotomy." I yell to an empty room.

AAAAAAAAAHHHHHHHHHHHHHHHHHHHHHHHH-HH !!!!!!!

**The Keynote**

A driver takes me to the hotel, where conferences like these are held within small, discreet chambers, surrounded by a vibey cocktail lounge and dimly lit patio.

Before my keynote speech, I really look at myself in the full length bathroom mirror. These past six months of sleepless nights after fighting with Conor, on top of sleepless nights of developing my thesis, have given me exactly one gray hair, two puffed up under eye bags, and a dozen new wrinkles. My skin is sallow, pale. I look *too thin* all of a sudden. What the fuck? You know, I enjoy being skinnylicious, but.. in this staunchly truthful mirror, I look like shit. It dawns on me that the weight I've been losing perhaps isn't achievement oriented at all, but a byproduct of stress.

I take out my phone and pull up pictures of myself from the beginning of this year, and pictures from last. It haunts me. I haunt myself, a pallid pink-haired ghost.

"Ugh." I mutter to myself, and reapply an orange tinted lip gloss that plumps my lips. I spray some hair product.. arrgg-hhhhhu8hhh811.........ocv6iô{{
{
}

I look at my notes. It doesn't matter that I look my best tonight – the presentation has to be the aesthetic center. I just have to look a marginal amount of put together. Clean, smart, tailored.

When I get up to the stage, I repeat my performance from last night. A two-night presentation on the Lattice: an emerging neural linking program that helps merge coding and DNA through biotechnological devices, creating a possibility for the implantation of consciousness. For an hour and a half, I meticulously pore through my research as several dozen of my peers, fellows, and mentors look on. I thought I got another flirty little wink from Dr. Porcellian, but now I realize that he has a tic that causes him to wink when he thinks someone just made a good point.

Dazzle with supervenience.
Illuminate the links between technology and spirituality.
Neuromorphic computing and quantum immortality.

Yes, a lot of my research is buzzworded to oblivion to attract the attention of scholars, investors, and patrons, but in core of it, the science is sound.

After my speech, I go with some of the others to the cocktail lounge, where there is a fundraiser-type of mixer or something of the sort, an afternoon of happy hour social calls where my peers can get drunk, hang out, and talk nerdy.

Gerard comes up to me asking, "What's the gossip?"
"I got nothing. You?"
"I got some tea on the wife's mental institution stay."
"What's the tea?"
"Remember what I told you the other day? I guess they want to keep her in there for a little while longer, and they're working on getting a pass for our consciousness models to work with her."
"Damn."
"Alright, I gotta go home. My husband will be pissed if I miss tonight's movie night. I haven't had a real night at home in weeks."
"I know. This shit gets hectic. Have a good one."
"Later. Good job tonight, by the way."

Gerard leaves. I hesitate a little to go home to my boyfriend, who's been de facto living in my apartment even though he has his own place. We still haven't figured out a way to merge lives, this is evident even in location. I sit down with a strong martini by myself, decompressing in a corner underneath a slipshodly drawn portrait of a large green cat that has the phrase "Opportunity is the intersection of an idea and a customer" in a comically bold font.

"This is very 'graphic design is my passion.'"
A girl laughs looking at the cat image and sits down next to me. She introduces herself as Ariel.

We talk shop for a while – she is a researcher at Porcellian Labs as well, in a different sector. I like Ariel. I'm drawn to her right away. Tall, lean, long dark hair, deep dark brown eyes. She's friendly, has this over-familiarity and invasion of personal space that normally I would find annoying in others – for some reason, from her, I find it very charming. Her soft voice and gentle energy are betrayed by this in-your-face countenance. How can someone be at once so delicate and so aggressive?

She tells me about her vision for freezing a person's consciousness while they are still alive, and can be both frozen and living at once – cryogenics for the mental plane. It hasn't yet been fleshed out, but it will be.

She wants to take it to Dr. Porcellian one day and cites my research as an inspiration for her own developmental model.

"I love your work so much, you're really a star." Ariel gushes.
"Thank you. I love yours as well, I respect the dedication to your thesis. It's really cool, the freezing thing."
"Hahaha – cool! I get it!"
"Hahahah pun not intended."

"Well, yours is literally game changing. It's changing the game as we speak. You really think we can successfully implant consciousness?"
"Oh yeah."
"Because if we can isolate a consciousness, we can keep it on ice for the future."
"How I wish we could keep everything on ice for the future.."

Suddenly I can no longer focus on my theories and experiments. Something has struck me, and I'm flooded with thoughts about Conor and his unhappiness. I wish I could freeze time and freeze making this decision, selfish as that would be. A sexy suspended animation. A stasis. I wish I could give him what he wants, but I can't. Not at this time. I'm breaking his heart by stalling, and he's already moving on, implementing an exit strategy.

"What's wrong angel?" Ariel looks concerned.
"Umm. I don't know it might be nothing, but maybe it's not nothing. I found something on my boyfriend's phone. From a woman.."
"Is he cheating on you?"
"If he is, it's emotional cheating. It doesn't sound like they've met.. yet."
"Is she pretty?"
"Yes, very, from the looks of it.. On the.. Little picture."
"She can't be as pretty as you. You're fucking gorgeous."

When Ariel tells me that I laugh a little, then start to cry.

"Aww no, babe, don't cry."
>| Nooo don't kill yourself your too sexy ahah

She brushes a strand of hair out of my face and tucks it behind my ear. She shushes me and pats my head. I comply without speaking, completely submitting to her care. My head tilts down, but my eyes look up at hers. We share a gaze. Her eyes are hypnotic, I can't stop gazing. So soft. So pretty. Her lips part. Either in the flash of a split second, or in agonizing slow motion that freezes time, she kisses me.

When I was first hired at Porcellian Labs, I was known as Crypto Christy. I was a little famous (or infamous) in my field for knowing exactly when and how much to buy, hold, and sell. I had made obscene amounts of money that way. I was a shark. My obsession with digital currency took hold really after my last breakup, the bicoastal dude I dated in my last serious relationship before Conor. We had a painful, nasty, messy, closureless split when I wanted more than he could give – I wonder if what's happening now is a crucible headed towards karmic retribution. When I was with bicoastal boy I was working at the small but prestigious Silph Labs researching psychedelic therapy and clinical models of male personality disorder treatment. My research was published all over. I had siphoned drugs from the lab in a week-long bender to try to get over the breakup.

"Where's daddy's medicine?"
"I need closure!"

One night during that bender I came to the clinic fucked up, to the shock of my coworkers – and to my own shock, I discovered I was pregnant with my ex's baby. Dr. Blaise performed an emergency termination in his own office and sent me home to recover. As an asset to the clinic, I had a month of paid leave. I had always been a star in my field. Highly competent in my work, highly dysfunctional in my personal life. It was during that month of recuperation and deep introspection that I dreamed up my own working model of intrapersonal consciousness implantation. I wished that someone, something else could take over my mind at that time. Someone stronger than me whose strength I could equip to mitigate my anxiety, depression, dysfunction. A neural personality helper to guide me.

I went back to Silph Labs armed with this new developing horizon. No boys, no breakups, just me with blinders on diving into work. I was poached from Silph Labs by Porcellian Labs when a paper I had published on consciousness and subjectivity caught the eye of Dr. Porcellian himself. Together, we developed a tool for crafting new nets of personality, tulpas, giving artificial beings real human consciousness. It would be called The Humanization Procedure, and it was going to change the world. The device programmed to do this was my Lattice. It would download onto a false carbon chassis, a real human-based personality. The work was done in secret underground and I had to sign a hell of an NDA to participate. It wasn't exactly ethical, but then again is any science when it first begins?

The kind of money I was making at Porcellian made my crypto endeavors pale in comparison. I bought a second-floor apartment in the heart of the city. My wardrobe alone was worth six figures. I bought antique swords. I adopted two cats, Dollar and Diamond. A fancy round bed with LED lights. A tv stand with LED lights. Drawers with LED lights that contained thousands of dollars of the best lingerie money can buy. I hired staff to clean and cat sit. I automated my daily tasks with programs. I put my money where my mouth is – lip filler, dental work, diamond jewelry on my ears and neck to highlight my nasolabial thirds, bringing to life my once-dull pout.

**The First Date**

A few months into officially starting to bring to life my theories on the Humanization Procedure, getting the ball rolling on initial experiments and hush-hush speaking events,
I met Conor. I don't know why our paths crossed, but they
did. Call it fate.

He had just gone on a string of unsuccessful dates and was
going to give up on love completely, relegate himself to just
being lonely. I realized.. I was lonely too. Very much so,
actually. What good is having a view from the top with no
one to share it with?

While we laughed together, I touched his arm. I invaded his
personal space.
I liked him.

"So what do you do?" he asked me.
"I'm a scientist."
"That's cool, what kind of science?"
"It's kinda hard to explain. It's almost like philosophy. I'm
a philosopher."
"Try me."
"I can't really talk about some of it cause I signed an NDA,
but here's a little outline of the stuff I can show you." I get
out my digital dossier and show him the preliminary notes.
"Fuck yeah, damn that's interesting."
"I know. What about you, what do you do?"

We were immediately obsessed with each other. It was euphoric. It was chemical. It was magical. Call it illumination.

"Are you going to walk me home and make sure I get home
safe?"
"Yes." He held my hand as he walked me home.

"This is my building, want to come up?"
"Wow, your place is insane."
"I know."

We sat on the floor in my living room as I poured us a fancy pink wine into holographic stems. I suddenly became very aware of the fabric of my button up Prada shirt. How crisp and stiff and white it was. Every corner, pressed immaculately. The everythingness, the allatonceness, the hyperawareness. How I had just touched his arm in the hotel lobby flirtatiously, how his clothes were softer than mine. How my eyeliner was precise. How my skirt, also Prada, didn't have a single stain or wrinkle. How his glasses had this attractive asymmetry, and even his wallet was dented and unkempt. How my hair, bizarrely, didn't move, but his hair waved in the wind where there was none indoors, defying physics. I knew exactly what was about to happen. I just knew.

And I was suddenly so fucking excited.

Defying all logic, all science, all reason, I just knew – and yet I was still taken aback when he kissed me. Partial illumination. In that moment, I was so present, so there, more present than any other moment in my life leading up till then – yet at the same time, it felt dissociative, like my perception was leaving my body. When he touched my hair, when he put his tongue in my mouth, when he pressed my body into his – I was in the moment, and I was in another world.

"Are you real?"

I was on top of him, and he pulled me up so that I was sitting, stradding him, woman on top like I always am. He'd have the perfect view of my body. I bent down to keep kissing him.

He started unbuttoning my shirt, emboldened and unrestrained. His hands all over my body, lifting my skirt.

"Oh my god, what the fuck.. Your thong says Philosopher?"
"Yeah, I told you I'm a philosopher."
"This is unreal."
"I know."

**The Gift**

Back in the present moment, the time travel of a kiss, Ariel has pressed her lips deeply into mine.

"Thanks, I needed this." I whisper when she pulls away. I give her a little kiss on the cheek.
"Hee hee.. now you and your boyfriend are even." She giggles.
"Nah, I don't believe in keeping score like that.. but you know what I think.. I think.. it will sure make him happy if I bring you home tonight. He's always had a fantasy about me and another girl. You interested?"

After seeing Conor's mystery woman phone notification, I become obsessed with having a sexual encounter of my own. I stumble upon Ariel, flirt with her, even let her kiss me, but the guilt of not sharing this with Conor makes me want to pull him into this. This isn't just a sexual encounter of my own, this can be a sexual encounter of our own.

Ariel takes a moment to think over my deliciously naughty suggestion, and a sort of illegal-looking smile crosses her face.
"Oh I can be down.. but.. Is it bad that I want to keep you all for myself? I'm not into men as much as girls."
"Tonight I'm afraid we'll have to share. Also, you know, my boyfriend's kind of girly."
"Girly?"
"I mean, like, in touch with his feminine side. In a hot way. He's hot."
"Have you done this before?"
"Um, once in college," I reply, running out of brainpower and vocabulary. "It was hot."
"Ok, so you have some experience in kinky stuff."
"Quite a bit," I divulge, now a little shy. "Before I ever

worked in this lab, I was an escort and dominatrix to pay my way through grad school."
"How exciting!"
"Well, it was just a thing. Not good or bad, just a thing."

I don't discuss my past in sex work very often, but something about her makes her feel like a nonjudgmental space. It's refreshing. I want to hear more from her. And it seems like she wants to express more to me..

"Hey, I have a proposition of my own to share. Later tonight, there's going to be a.. gathering.. in a private residence, and I'm to be one of the sexual performers, kind of like a submissive on display while the attendees whip and spank and so on. They're always looking for girls, too. Would you want to come?"
"I'd love to check it out. Should I bring Conor too?"
"No, you come alone or with me. They take the guest list very seriously." She suddenly looks stern and solemn. "Girls they can display, who are vetted by performers like me, they allow on a day's notice. But the consequences for men are dire. I do have an extra invitation to the party, for you, here."

She reaches into her polished black blazer and hands me a small black slip of paper with a handwritten address and the word "Leonore" scrawled in the center. I put it in my Prada bag.

"This sounds pretty severe, is there a dress code?" I ask.
"Whatever you're wearing now is fine. you won't be wearing much later."
"I know that's right.." I laugh. I notice a black paper on the floor by my feet. "Oh hey, I think you dropped your invitation."
"Damn, I gotta be careful with these pockets. Thank you."

"Shall we?"

I beckon her home, where I present her to Conor lustfully. We enter my apartment seductively, messily, hornily taking off each other's jackets and teasing the collars of our blouses.

"Hey babe! What's going on?" he calls out.
"Babe you know how you always fantasized about me and another girl? This is your lucky moment!"

Maybe they can both dominate me tonight.
The night is young.

"What?! Oh my goddd.. so this is what you meant when you texted me you got me a surprise gift."
"Mhmmm. Oh yes. Don't you have the day off tomorrow? You can party."
"Don't you not?" he asks me. "You can't be out late, naughty girl."
"Hmm, I'll call in sick."
"Don't make me laugh! You never call in sick."

I kiss him to shut him up. Strutting towards the kitchen, I bring three beers out for everyone. We drink on the couch. There's an atmospheric playlist in the background.

I sit in between Ariel and Conor, wedging myself between them like a nestled hen in a horny henhouse. Like something out of a movie, they take turns kissing me and touching my hands, my neck, my chest. My entire body reacts all at once.

I enjoy the hand-kissing, and they almost side by side deposit kisses up my arm and on my neck. Further down my exposed collarbone, the skin is sensitive and dreamy. It makes me giggle being touched there. They each remove one half of my button-down shirt, exposing my bare chest, and they both grab one of my breasts. The sensation, and how synced they are for having just met, almost makes me crack up.

"Oh my god, you guys, this is so cinematic.." I moan.

"Shhh.." in coordination, they shush me. Conor kisses my mouth wide open, passionately circling his tongue into my mouth. Then Ariel kisses me, biting my lip playfully. Then I watch them kiss each other. I bite my lip into the lens of the invisible camera haunting my imagination. A spectral seduction.

"What do you want to do?" I whisper into Conor's ear, "This is for you."
"I just want to do you. Everything else is an afterthought."

Continuing their synchronized movements, Ariel and Conor trail their hands up my skirt. I'm wet, so wet. Their fingers slide in and out of me. I run my hands through their hair, grab their necks, grope them. With one hand, I hold Conor's hand to Ariel's breasts like I want to possess her entire body through him. With my other hand, I unbutton his pants. I lose my mind trying to keep track of all the movement. I can't take much more, and fighting the urge to moan louder, I squiggle out of their grasp, put my legs up in the air and back down, giggling.

Ariel takes over and straddles me. She starts to unbutton her shirt, the first few buttons peeling away to reveal a tiny black heart tattoo between her cleavage.

"So pretty.." I say breathlessly. I unbutton the rest of her shirt as she weaves her dainty hands through my hair, twirling pink ringlets. I throw her shirt onto the floor and meander to her skirt, starting to unzip her zipper. Giving her a look that asks for confirmation, she locks eyes with me and nods. She licks her lips. I bite mine. She stands up and lets me take her skirt off. I get on my knees in front of her. The underwear perching on her slim hips are a ruffled blue silk number that I stop to feel, enjoying its textile, before I take them down. Her black pubic hair is shaved into the shape of a heart above a perfect, smooth pussy. I gasp.

"You're just pretty everywhere, aren't you?"
"I taste pretty, too."
"Wait tho –" I oscillate between gasping and laughter. I pull up my skirt to show her that I too have a heart above my pussy, but mine is pastel pink, to match my hair. Just above and to the left of my hair I have a tiny pastel pink heart tattoo. Two hearts. Matching heart tattoos. It's so synchnorously slutty.

"Oh my god, you're gonna make me even wetter." She moans.
"You should feel how wet you make me."
"I wanna eat your heart out."
"No, me first."

I give Conor a lustful look as he is sitting on the couch admiring us, taking in the view.

"Fuck me." I demand him.

On my knees, I trace Ariel's perfect heart and kiss around it. I look back at Conor, undressing quickly to reveal his springloaded erect cock. His hands are on my hips, grabbing my ass through my skirt, fingering my pussy. He tears the last of my clothes off.

"Yeah, she's fucking wet." He tells Ariel, who smacks her

lips.

"You both did this to me. It's your fault."
"You're a naughty girl and you need to be fucked like one."
Conor grabs his cock and with a swift motion thrusts it in
my dripping wet tight pussy. I gasp loudly and turn around
to look at him, but before I can say anything, he tells me to
shut up.

"Shut up and enjoy it, my dirty little slut."
"Yes boss.." I whisper plaintively, and turn my attention
back to Ariel's cunty heart. I split her lips with my tongue
as Conor fucks me senseless, thrusting over and over and
over and o v e r. He reaches his hand over and strokes my
clit, distracting my brain and my mouth. I moan through
pussy juice. Like a movie, like a fucking porno, we all finish
at the same time, and I feel cum soaking my back and my
ass where he has just pulled out.

"Fuck. Holy shit."

I stumble over to the kitchen island. Sweating, stumbling,
giddy, I grab a towel and a bottle of water. Ariel gulps it
down as Conor wipes me off. I can't stop giggling.

We're panting on the floor, drinking water.

"If I could freeze this moment in time.." I muse.
"Oh, if only we had the technology." Ariel reflects, laugh-
ing.

We linger in the afterglow for a few delicious minutes, silently splayed on the couch. Just limbs. No thoughts to ruin
the moment. Freeze. Save the game.

The clothes that were so chaotically torn off, clutter on the floor as we all catch our breath. Ariel swiftly gets dressed.

"This was so fun! I gotta go. See you later." With a wink, Ariel hurriedly sweeps on her jacket and heads out the door.

Once the door closes, it takes me a moment, but I see it – the invitation that fell out of her jacket. She must have forgotten to check her pockets. Laying at the foot of the couch next to the pile of clutter, it looks unimposing and innocent.

Ignoring it, I take a quick shower. I freshen up my makeup and brush my hair.

"What are you doin?" Conor, still fully nude, asks me as I lay out some clothes on my bed. "You goin out?"

"Yeah, I have a work party I wanted to go to."
"This wasn't enough of a party for you?" he chuckles.
"Oh, this was a party, most definitely. But I was invited to this girls thing from work and I kinda feel like it would be cool. Shouldn't be too late."
"Should I come with?"
"Oh I'd love that but it's kind of a girl thing."
"Okay have fun."
I kiss him on the lips. "I hope you have a chill, mellow night. Love you."
"Love you too."

He gets in the shower. I put on a slutty outfit, throw a coat on, and get in my car.

**The Party**

I park my car a few blocks away and huddle in my fur coat as I click clack down the streets at night. Underneath my coat, a light blue Bordelle strappy number ornately decorates my pale, milky body. What a fancy neighborhood, to my surprise. I was expecting a large warehouse, some kind of rave dungeon, but it's a lone suburban mansion, the only house on the street. From the outside, it looks inconspicuous. Whatever sexual escapades are going on there, you'd never know. The invite says to go in through the back. I walk through an alley. At the door, a huge man in a ripped white ruffled top and tuxedo jacket guards.

"Hey, I'm one of the girls for tonight's party." I tell him about my invitation.

"Invite?"
"Ah, shit.." I dig through my pockets, "I left it in my car."

"Password?" he grumbles, like a pirate. I give a sultry whisper: "Leonore".

"Ehh.. that checks, I'll let ya slide this time."

He opens the door slightly. A crack of magnificent pink light seeps through.

"Wow," I gasp quietly.

"Just wait a sec," he stops me. "I need to see you turn off your devices. There is no recording allowed."

"What if I need to get into contact with someone?"
"If they're here, you'll find them. Or they'll find you. Respect the process."

"Sure thing." I disengage all my devices and walk on through.

The door opens into a marvelous art deco atrium, a vast expanse with lightless chandeliers in a champagne pink hue. Ostrich feather boas in ornate designs decorate the walls. The atrium is lit with candles. A soft aesthetic, the only LEDs are pink and purple. Halo lighting. Bouquets of peony and lily on iridescent tables. Is this what heaven looks like?

Angels walk around, women in various states of undress, some coupled up, some throupled up, some grouped up, some solo like me, walking around bewildered. New girls, I guess. I survey the fits. A woman in a gold venetian mask covering her eyes, angel wings on her back. Two women both in tuxedos. A beauty naked except for a black leather cape and an armored plate covering her chest. An angel in a sheer white thong with marabou trim. Masked, caped, armored, a secret lair filled with beautiful women. Music bumps on the sound system, a thumping bass beat with orchestral crescendos that add to the intensity of the moment.

Exploring past the atrium, I walk through a hallway with multiple rooms for entertainment, and come to a main room, a crystal ballroom with a display case that's like a stage. It's too far for me to see, but it looks like the display is for staging sexual performances.

I open my coat slightly, teasing a peek at my pale blue straps. With the array of holographic lucite platforms and extravagant latex black thigh high stiletto boots, my modest pale blue Vivienne Westwood heels can't help feeling a little underdressed. Well, under-heighted. Ha.

A gaggle of Amazonian beauties flutter past me, a mirage of

showgirlesque sparkles and feathers.

There are very few men, and the ones that are – are either working at the party as staff, fully nude on all fours as stunning women walk them on leashes around the opulent grounds, or laid on top of tables with operatic displays of sushi on the man meat of their bodies. It is a game for the women, by the women, about the power of women.

"You were invited here," a masked brunette approaches me, "because you're powerful."

"This is.. incredible. Wow, thank you." I'm mesmerized and honored.

"You work hard, and you should play hard." She impishly tugs on my fur, letting it fall to show a pale blue stap. "Why don't you have some fun?"

"Why not indeed." I giggle. I scan the dazzling crowd for Ariel.

Of course. The center of it all. The crystal stage. There she is, looking up at it, enjoying the view. Mmmm mmm mmm, I think. Mama you look so good tonight it's damn sinful. She looks like an angel, bathed in light and caressed in nude latex. I get closer to the show. A curvy blonde is bent over on top of a wooden structure as a leather-nun-outfit-clad mistress strikes her ass with a riding crop.

I watch Ariel enjoying this ritualistic display. I desire to be displayed as well. I desire to be controlled. I desire to sub-mit. Just as I'm lost in a musing, at a loss of words, Ariel turns around to see me with a beaming smile.

"Oh my god you made it!! Yay!" She air kisses me on both

cheeks, mwah mwah.

"This is so amazing! I've never seen anything like it. It's like something out of a movie, for real."

"Hey," she takes my arm and shuttles me towards the front, "how'd you like to be in the show?"

"I.. I.. Really?.. wow.." I'm frazzled verbally, but Ariel recognizes the spark in my eyes that enthusiastically, curiously, desires.

She hands me over to the mistress who displays me, and I am a doll, a toy for the spectators. They can make me do whatever they want. No decision is mine to make. Finally, I can relinquish control. The mistress claps my booty cheeks.

I'm having such a great time, and once my turn is done on the display, I look for Ariel to tell her "Your turn!" But I don't see her anywhere.

Instead, to my surprise, I see Conor. What? How the fuck?

"Oh my god! How did you get in?"
"I found the invitation! I said I'm your plus one!"
"Really?" I kiss him, but I get this feeling that I am not allowed to. Seeing him here, worlds colliding of home and work, is unexpected and somehow even foreboding. I think about what Ariel said of men and dire consequences.. I remember but then I forget. We will have to find her, or get out of here.
"I showed the guy out front the invitation but it was weird, he gave me a cryptic warning, it was like some freemason vibes."
"Really? He let you in?"
"Yeah."

"Ok.." I slightly panic, trying to figure out what to do. "Have you seen Ariel?"

"No, I just caught the tail end of your crazy ass getting smacked by that whip."

"Ok let's go find her. We should probably get out of here."

Conor seems unfazed. I look around frantically, my heart thumping with the beat. I start to move towards an exit, tugging at his shirt. In that moment, the music stops playing. The pink lights shut off, and the candles, lit by LEDs, turn dark. Silence and darkness. A single spotlight flashes from the stage, seemingly searching the crowd. Whatever was about to happen, I had a sinking feeling it wasn't good.

Through the intercom, a stern woman's voice seethes.

"Never forget! We're women who have the power to create. But we also have the power.. to destroy."

Murmurs abound. Is it my imagination, or is the stage shaking?

"It has come to our attention that we have an interloper in our midst. One of our own has let this sacred event be tarnished. For that, there will be consequences."

No, it is not my imagination. The rumble of the voice shakes the stage.

"We have rules that are meant to be followed. It is strictly forbidden to break the rules. There will be consequences. The event, the impact, will alter everyone's reality."

As the voice repeats its phrases, each one becoming more cacophonous, echoic, multiplying into sonic overlays, the crystal stage shakes harder, and then the walls, and then

the ground. The mysterious earthquake shatters champagne
flutes, spills drinks, knocks women off their stilettos. Wom-
en screaming, some frozen in place, a few composed, like
they've seen this before. My shoes standing their ground,
strong in their low-heelness, kick Conor's ankles gently as
I tell him to move.

In the chaos, we somehow find Ariel. I clutch her shoulder
with one hand as the building shakes, holding Conor's hand
with my other.

"What the fuck is going on?"
"A sonic attack – you must leave! They found me out. Leonore was my personal password. They know. They know!"

"Fuck!" I declare helplessly, as I try to rush her out with us.
She remains steadfast and resists as panicking women clear
out from room to room. "Come on, let's get out of here,
please!"

"I'm sorry!" Ariel cries. "It's all my fault. I shouldn't have
brought you here. He never should have come here. Get out,
quick, while you still can. That way!"
"What about you?!?"
"I have to face what's coming."
"Please come with us."
"If I do that, they will come after you too. I have to keep
you safe."
"I'm scared! I'm scared for you."
"The consequences of my fate are none of your concern.
Now go!"

Ariel disappears, seamlessly running to a room in the back
of the cracked, torn stage. She must be sacrificing herself
so that me and Conor can safely get out. I'm tempted to
follow her, but Conor grabs me and we make our way

towards a side door, following a group of crying beauties, sequined tears floating down fearful faces. Skinny elbows push and shove me, and we barely slink through an exit door. A chaos of latex and feathers on the floor, reeking of spilled champagne. Cups, shoes, bags tattered on the grass of the courtyard. My coat flies off, joining the mess. I pant as I run. Conor's hand in mine, we finally speed through the mansion's gates and down the streets. I barely feel the cold, even in lingerie.

Stunned, shocked, bewildered, Conor and I look back at the mansion momentarily. It continues to shake. We run.

Coatless in the night, shoes half clacking off, I somehow regain cognition and trace my steps back to my car, those cold hard blocks of sidewalk.
"Did you drive, Conor? Did you park close by?"
"No, I took the tunnels."
"Okay, let's hurry home. Get in."

Hands shaking, I activate the ignition. A single strip of pale blue morning ends this dark night. I drive so fast into the frontispiece of daybreak, towards my apartment.

"These fucking people.. jeez it was so emasculating." He mutters.
"What are you talking about?"
"You know.. the guys. Jesus fucking christ."
"I thought it was kind of cool. Adored and objectified by hot women. Isn't that the future some guys want?"
"Not me."
I stay silent as I drive.

"You know, you know this about me, I'm more traditional. And you, you're so seamlessly engaged with modernity."
"..."

## Sliced

The next day Conor sleeps it off, and I skip work, calling in my first sick day in years. Things remain as they are. I find this slice of time to be the first we've gotten together in a while, to talk about our relationship.

My hands are cold. A haunting chill runs through them while I sweat. My mind cannot process, but the body knows. My mind wants to forget, but the body remembers. The body that just 24 hours ago was having one of the most pleasurable, viscerally euphoric experiences of its life, is now going through the most subtle, eerie wringer. You can't freeze time. Technology gives us illusions, but we will never have the genuine article. Maybe decades, centuries from now, humankind will be able to manipulate time, but for now, all we have is the illusions that our minds create. The memory is the medium.

I address the things I may have withheld. It's now or never. I give myself two minutes to breathe. It's time. I know what's about to happen, and I'm so fucking despondent. We need to talk. I start, and he continues.

"Do I really want a relationship where I have to choose between security and certainty?" he lectures. "Pure love is when you know what makes someone anxious, and you do what you can to ease that."

"Have I not been putting in my all, and doing what I can to make you happy and calm? Conor, I love you, and I hope you see how much I love you."

"We saw a woman possibly die last night, and we saw a remote device trigger a seismic event. The trials of artificial intelligence are disastrous. The woman who died, is it her consciousness we'll be implanting? This.. form of embalming? What is the ethical code of consciousness implantation? Dead or alive?"

"I don't see what that has to do with us."

"How are you so good at compartmentalizing? What the hell kind of science was this?" he laments. "This is all too much! This all makes no sense! Christina, what are you thinking??"
"I've been thinking, it was.. I think we've gotten really close and I've been loving that. I would like to push this forward in the way you want. I won't push you away when you talk about our future"
"I won't talk about this any more."
"Are you serious?"
"Frankly, I've said all I have to say about this."

I try to ease this, I try to apologize.
He gives me a monologue, and he leaves me.
"I'm embarrassed, I feel all the negative emotions toward myself for trying so hard at this thing."

"What are you talking about?" I respond, exasperated. "Like I haven't tried hard? No matter how hard I've tried, even if it failed, I would never feel embarrassed about putting my all into a relationship."

"I've just done so much more, gave so much more, tried to make you see things my way, and it's pretty clear that the things that haven't been working between the two of us, are not changing."

"But you've made me see things differently, and reconsider. I do, I want to be a mother. I understand now, what is important." I whispered quietly, flatlining – I could feel the insincerity in my voice, and so could he. "It would be selfish of me to make you stay. I wish I could make you happy and I want you to be happy and get what you want. I'm sorry it couldn't be with me. I'm sorry I couldn't be that person for you."

It doesn't matter what I say. Nothing I can say can change his mind.

"I'm sorry."

It's a conversation from me to me. He now mostly stays silent. He's 'said all he has to say'. My heart sliced in a thousand different ways with the blade of rejection. And then he takes the knife out of my chest,

"I think we should break up."

I had no idea he was that unhappy. Usually in a breakup I could see it coming a mile away, but not this. I mean I did but.. It feels so sudden. Like he dislocated me mentally and I have no anchor.

"I guess my apology to you is.." he trails, "I'm sorry that I thought I could change you into seeing things my way. I thought that you would come around. But I don't want you to be pressured into anything, and you're way too strong willed for that. You're too perfect."

I have a Prada backpack that looks perfect and flawless from the outside, excellent condition. But inside, there are rips in each pocket, which things fall though down into the bottom, and make a mess.

It's never enough, is it? Society wants girls to be strong. Men nowadays want girls to be strong, independent.

But is there such a thing as too strong? Too independent? It becomes too much. I'm that independent, assertive woman you wanted. But now my independence threatens my personal life.

Maybe it isn't my destiny to be settled down in a relationship, maybe the orthodox way of living is not for me. Maybe it's not meant to be for me to have a cute little family, a slow life. Maybe Dollar and Diamond are enough for me. It's my destiny to show up for something bigger and make change in the world. The sacrifice, the pain, the way my personal life suffers, that's the pain of my girlhood.

Darling, I wish you could let me be me. You like how fun I am, how creative and intelligent I am. What's wrong with waiting a few more years? My freedom, the freedom you love so much, will be stifled by a child and a home. I love you. I love my work too. I put my all into my work and I'm changing the game, I'm just getting started. Can't it be both?

Being a girlboss is lonely. Zero illumination.

We have no idea where the world will go. I don't think about bringing a child into it. I think about bringing my art, my science, into it.

The last thing he says to me,
"I truly wish you the best, and I will always love you. You are better off without me. I'll stop torturing you now."

So with that, he leaves.

This wasn't a breakup. This was a fucking eulogy.

I'm composed and perfect on the outside, but on the inside,

I'm a mess. I cry into my Prada backpack.

I just can't make it good. An hour passes. Nothing feels good. Everything feels bad. Life doesn't feel real. I'm starting to understand the Dr's wife's mental breakdown. The wife had an affair and a subsequent descent into madness – the shock, the guilt, the trauma, damaged her so, that she couldn't piece herself back together again. He tried many things, all of which failed, so eventually he sent her to an institution for the clinically insane. To this day, he continues to attempt experimental curative technologies, which everyone silently knows are the center, the heart, of our work at the labs. He loves her that much. Love is pain, isn't it?

**Gerard**

In the blur of these post-apocalyptic days, I write letters to Gerard.

I usually text, but I feel compelled to put words to paper. It feels more formal, more official. Occasionally, ever so faintly, in the caverns of my mind there is a looming stalactite threatening to drop on me with a "write your will" "suicide note" "what is there to live for?" and I sigh as I spelunk into that cavern, for shattering those thoughts into oblivion is a herculean task.

How fast the minutes go. How slow the minutes go. Moments of decognition. I forget where the cat shit goes and scoop it into the kitchen sink instead of the toilet bowl. Bursting into tears, I think: 'at least it wasn't the closet'.

I ruminate, who is going to care of my cats, and of me, when I can't take care of myself? I keep thinking about the wife's mental breakdown. It haunts me.

The first day I walked into the facility, I met with the Dr and a man was sitting in his office, tapping on a rose gold laptop. His grey T shirt read: "everyone wants to fuck a retard till they get to the asylum." The Dr introduced him as Gerard Evans, lead programmer. He would go on to become my best friend.

"You two will be working together on the development of our consciousness models."
Dr. Porcellian gave a brief overview of our first assignment and left the room. I tried to make conversation as Gerard furiously typed with a laser focus.

"Nice to meet you, I'm Christina."

"Sup." He answered flatly.

"Nice shirt."

"Yea."

"Nice ring," I noticed a flashy silver band around his ring finger. "You married?"

"Engaged. Dan and I will be getting married next month." A furtive glance, a sideways grin. So he isn't impenetrable.

"You seeing anyone? Any drama?" he asked me.

"No, not at the moment."

"It's probably easier for this type of job. You already know, what we do is demanding. Not that much time for a personal life."

"What's your secret? How do you make it work?"

"I'm a scientist, he's an artist. We both work a lot, and we want the same things. It's simple, really. We just aligned. When you know, you know."

Over the next month as I became friends with my coworker, I received an invite to my first gay wedding.

Gerard and Dan's wedding was beautiful. Simple, small, tasteful. They honeymooned in Spain for a week before returning to their jobs in full force. It made me believe that I too could find love despite being married to my work.

All the men who have entered and exited my life, Gerard was the one of the few who consistently stayed.

In my time working at the facility, I had another ex, a quirked-up old-money white boy I broke it off with. We didn't speak for a year, nothing at all, and one day months of silence later he sent me a cryptic text. I became afraid that he would try to stalk me or something. You never know what's going on in crazy people's minds, especially if they're scorned. I confided in Gerard how unnerved I was at that text. What if he finds me? What if tries to hurt me?

"What is he gonna do, grumble at you in his fancy boots? Flex on you in his Gucci jacket?" Gerard laughed.
I laughed too. Levity is the slayer of anxiety.

Blocked and moved on.

In truth, being a girl is scary, no matter how strong and independent and bossy we may be. All my strength training, all my weapons, all my self-defense skills aside.. it would still be easy to overpower me, to catch me off guard. Even though I am always on guard. Beneath my strong independent exterior lies a deep, hidden layer of PTSD.

Speaking of crazy people. Back to Mrs. Porcellian's nervous breakdown.

"What happened?" I once asked Gerard.

"Listen," he replied, "I'm going to tell you a story."

"Once upon a time, there was a beautiful princess living in a humble village. Really, she was a peasant, but in her heart, she knew she was meant for something bigger. She wanted to be a princess and longed for a prince to save her from the squalor of her humble village. Every night she prayed, to find love, to cultivate her beauty and charm so well that it would allure the most dashing of princes and find a love that would bring happiness, heartwarming, and heirs.

The peasant was all alone, and she spent day and night working hard to build a life for herself worthy of a princess. She dreamed that one day all this hardship, all this struggle, would one day be for something. An enterprising princess, she crawled and crawled her way out of the village and into her own beautiful tower.

Men from all over the lands and far away caught sight of her beauty, sent her coin and scrolls and presents until her tower blossomed. Oh, but the endless work carried with it an underside of traumatizing burnout. Over time, the princess became tired from the immense amount of work it took to maintain her tower. It weighed on her, a heavy diadem on her delicate little head. She needed help. She went to bed at night crying, and she woke up to the day wanting to sleep. Exhausted from doing everything herself her whole life, the princess took a break from the duties of strongholding her tower, and went on a fated date with a dashing prince.

The prince and princess had an exciting courtship, filled with romance, chemistry, and connection. Birds were singing, colors were brighter. She thought she had finally found true love. She went to sleep at night smiling, and she woke up to greet the day with euphoria.

So blinded by that chemistry and romance, the princess lost sight of the bigger picture. The prince, from a prominent family of the kingdom by the sea, dazzled the princess with promises of future adventures. She was under his spell. But the prince didn't want a peasant for a princess. He was not of the mind to provide for her. He did not want heirs. Over time, it only drained her energy. It slowly drained her beauty, her sleep, her health, her smile, without her noticing. When the princess realized this and broke free of the dazzling romantic spell, she left him.

As it turns out, she didn't need a prince – she needed a king. A strong, masculine man who could provide and lavish. Why have a prince, when I struggle the same as I do alone, she thought. It will be hard, but I will endure.

So she endured. She daydreamed. She recovered her energy back. It took time.

And one day, she found her king. He gave her everything she could ever need, he was the sturdy circlet in which the delicate diamond of her beauty was set. No flimsy discount bin chain here. He let her be weak, dainty, feminine, like she was meant to. He was her container. His masculine strength dovetailed with her fragile girlish countenance. He wanted heirs – with her. More than anything, he saw and understood her. She was so elated and grateful. She bloomed. She did not wilt. She wanted to make him the happiest king of all the lands. With the king, the princess was happier, healthier, safer, more secure. The fertile princess produced two beautiful heirs for him. It was her happily ever after. He made her a queen.

But the princess made a mistake – she went back to the prince. On a side quest one day, she encountered the prince.. and alas, his dashing charm seduced her once again. She did something she thought she could never do. Their whirlwind romance reignited, and the princess betrayed the king.

The princess was aghast at herself – why did she self-sabotage? Why wasn't it enough? Did she feel unworthy of happiness? What was she doing? Questions erupted in her head like a horde of demons. The princess self-destructed. 'Why did I do this?' She thought and ruminated over and over again. 'Is it because I do not think I deserve love and security and happiness? I keep repeating my psychodrama because I am so familiar with chaos? Will I ever let myself be happy? Am I doomed to wallow in my sadness? Am I doomed to wallow in my sadness? Am I doomed to wallow in my sadness? Do I not deserve good things? Do I not deserve happiness? Do I not deserve love? Do I not deserve a good life?'

The king sent the princess to a healing fortress in the east to get her mind right. He moved his kingdom to save his queen. But every trick he had up his sleeve, every wizard and sorceress and potion and elixir and ritual in an attempt to tip the scales of her sanity, had failed. After each futile attempt, he moved his kingdom back to the west, where it could flourish as his royal court continue to toil over a method to save her from herself. East or west, her self-persecution rests.

So there she is, there she remains, locked in another tower.

Do you get what I am saying?"

## The Birth of Clarence

A day goes by.
Another day.
A weekend.
A week.
Another weekend.

Bitcoin is up again. I don't really care. Do you?

I'm so tired. I can hardly get out of bed. Even the smallest tasks feel daunting. Head in my hands at the edge of the bed, I'm so overwhelmed.

Some days I just shut down. I decline. I plateau. The LEDs that surround my rooms feel like they lost their luster. Colors lose their brightness. Life loses its saturation. An idea would die of sheer loneliness in my brain right now.

Ten thousand ideas would die in a massacre of oversaturation distress in the asylum of my brain right now.

On the bed, contemplating. On the $8,000 dollar round bed with the quilted headboard, vaping lightly. Lingerie doesn't feel fun to wear anymore. The lace appliques, the neon sets, they lose their luster too.

There is a blankness, a confusion. Am I not feminine enough? Is all that is my femininity reliant on my reproductive ability – or rather, desire? Is this why Conor left me?

What of my polished, girly looks? It's another full time job to keep them up. It's another full time job yet to keep up a relationship. Well, I'm unemployed.

The soft blanket, printed in pastel blue clouds, gets grimy

and sticky with sweat as I bed rot into the night. I come from the kitchen and bed rot into the night. Crumbs in the bed as I mindlessly crunch ruffled potato chips, and nothing else. I expand my food palette, ordering takeout right to me. The only time I get up is to pee, and feed Dollar and Diamond. The only time I feel alive is when Dollar and Diamond cuddle up next to me, letting me pat them. They're saving what's left of my life. The prodigal childless cat lady has risen. Let her cook.

The positive of eating is it will help my hair grow. My hair, like my relationship, hasn't grown in almost a year. Starvation has an anesthetic effect that I abused like a painkiller to numb the hurt.

What of my polished eyeliner, my perfectly applied crimson lips? My makeup drawer is in shambles, spilling out in my cabinets. Towels scatter on the heated bathroom floor, stained with my fading pink hair dye. Brown roots burst through my crown.

Historically after my breakups I have gone through a period of right after, feeling this unexplained horniness and hypersexuality.

After bicoastal boy ghosted me, I wanted him so bad and sat in my car on my lunch break with my hand down my pants.

After I broke up with stalker boy, I sat in my office feeling waves of sex flashbacks tingle down my body.

After I told Conor I wanted a break in our relationship, the one and only time we had a proto-breakup, I woke up in my bed in this unreal pocket of the morning where I was disgustingly, indignantly, deliciously, embarrassingly wet, to the point where as soon as my fingers touched the seam of my panties I would soak them through. Monday morning masturbation ritual.

In the liminal space where we got back together and before we broke up for good, we had the best sex we've ever had. I wonder if any of our sexual memories live on in his mind as much as in mine. In my car, him going down on me, hands holding down my ankles as I writhe. Making out in the dark booth of an emo night themed bar, my hands trailing all over his body and wandering down his shirt, sneaking grabs of his boner through his pants. On my living room floor with my shirt unbuttoned and my skirt still on, bouncing me on his cock. Tying me in pink rope while I'm dressed in a slutty fairy outfit on Halloween, wings and glitter and a blonde wig, having his way with me and gagging my mouth with my own panties and fucking me rough. Blindfolding me and sensually, slowly, gently exploring my body, kissing my face, feeling how my nipples respond to his touch, investigating every fold of my pussy. Putting his cock in my mouth and finishing down my throat, making eye contact as I swallowed. "I love you so much it fucks me up."

But after this breakup, knowing it's for good and the love still lingering, my sex drive became nonexistent. The erasure of my libido, erasure of the joys of life. I didn't expect this.

I open my eyes and I look at you. I close my eyes and try to picture you and nothing comes up.

Moving on is never easy. Trying to practice non attachment, it's downright torture. Where did I go wrong? That my boyfriend was so unhappy with me, that he left. That I was too unserious, that every time he said he pictured this idyllic future with me, I recoiled or I shot it down. Or I tried to change him, to nurture a seed of uncertainty where he was fully leaning in, fully certain. I was just not ready to deepen things in that way. It's not that I didn't love him, I loved him dearly. But some concessions could not be made.

I can't sleep at night. When I do, I dream of earthquakes and fires. The sleep paralysis demon puts a ring on my finger. I wake up. She said no!!!!!!!

He wanted to wife me up. I wasn't comfortable with the idea of marriage, I couldn't picture myself as a wife or mother. Truthfully, I've never really thought much about it. The focal point of life was always about work and achievement for me. I'm cracking. By cracking, that's how the light gets in.

Can you love someone more than you've ever loved anyone in your entire life, and not know if you want to marry them, be with them for life, consider them the one?

Am I commitment phobe? Am I selfish? Is life just a vacation for me?

Fuck you fuck you fuck you. People like me make confessions in the form of accusations.

Life is raw, and it is new, and it is exhausting. It is constantly unfolding. There is an unyielding pressure to join it, at all times, at all costs.

"Wellness check on Park Ave." Gerard calls me. "How are you doing?"
"You know how."
"Still?"
"….."
"Girl. Pull yourself together."
"I don't know how."
"I do. We need you at work now. Come back, Christina."

"Why?"

"Because we've made progress."

"Of what variety?"

"Of the Project Clarence variety. It's yours. You need to main this. Have you heard of the dual consciousness response initiative?"

"I'm familiar."

"Tomorrow. It's straight up dog time."

He hangs up.

Distraught and trying to get pieces of his wife back from whence there were no longer, the Dr created a program that would both heal her and be her: strong like she was before, not fragile as she is now. This implanted consciousness will eventually be linked to her mind to regenerate her. In the interim, Clarence would need to be modeled after a healthier, stronger, savager consciousness. We give her the baseline of a female assassin. Pain tolerance, strength, regeneration, agility, intellect to think quickly on her feet. Situational awareness. Superior hearing and vision. Dexterity. Knowledge of basic weapons. Knowledge of basic human anatomy. But to balance out the severity of the assassin's consciousness, we would need to combine it with a more heartfelt, more human, subjectivity. This would be the base of her human form in the Humanization Process, with the assassin's skills as added mods.

"So who's the person we're basing Clarence's consciousness on?" I ask Gerard.

"Well, she was your idea, it's your little baby, so.. You."

I pause and smile. That's right.

"In a way, it was a positive that you took time off. It allowed us to study you. Even when you're broken like this, your subjectivity is stable and remarkably strong. This will be perfect for Clarence."

I can't help feeling validated. Finally, a silver lining.

"But for her own safety," he continues, "there is another woman who has the skills Clarence needs to survive successfully."

She was only known as 'X'. No one ever caught her, and few caught a glimpse of her. Many wondered if she was even real. But after a bullet was left behind at one of her crime scenes, one of many clandestine assassinations, Gerard and I knew she was real. An expert of survival. A master of life and death. A demi-goddess. Her prints and DNA matched no one in any system, so as far as the world of social tracking was concerned, she was a ghost. A perfect co-mother for Clarence.

I try to imagine what a day in the life of X must be like. It must be lonely.

I try to imagine what a day in the life of Mrs. Porcellian must be like. It must be agonizing. I can see why she needs something like Clarence when all other options for mental stability have been exhausted.

Clarence would need to first gain humanity before she could be linked to his wife.
Clarence would need to be built.

Code for respiratory system function. Code for immune system function. Cognition, memory, grace under pressure, it all has a variable. It all can be pinpointed. It can be crafted.

I wrote some of her very first lines of code. In fact, I wrote most of her code. Every line of my unique code contains a footprint of subjectivity, an imprint of myself I pass on to her. A gift. After all, Clarence is my baby, my precious darling masterpiece, and how could a fertile mother not pass some of her attributes onto her child?

28 → 10 [0]
= 102 → 3 [0]
> proactive debugging
{var greeting "good morning clarence" | var response "..."
S -6
P -4
A{
C
E "Emergence of an opposing viewpoint. New perspective on familiar circumstances. Birth. Childlike simplicity. N[-10]
}

Clarence would inherit something from me, a little slice of subjectivity. Entropy. Unpredictability. Raw emotion. When the humanization procedure reaches a certain per-cent, she will have agency. Something I have in abundance, that the Dr's wife never had a chance to have. The wife may be locked in a gilded cage, restrained from actions, but at the very least her mind and her thoughts are there.

>value distribution Q1 sum = 88 n→ 6 → 7
DNA CODONS {   991   309096 }  ♡♡
[green = true; orange = false]
{
exit status 1
>| TTT ATT TCT ACT AAT AGT
      TTC ATC GTT CTG GCG GGG
      CCG AAG AAA AGC CAT CAA } ...

Who am I to control Clarence's thoughts? She should have her own, be able to make her own choices. I suppose that is the dilemma of every scientist coding an artificial intelli-gence, or a parent debating whether or how much to enforce control over their children.

Clarence will have tasks, chores, functions. But how she chooses her function will eventually be completely up to her.

Clarence will encounter many challenges in her artificial life. It's my job to make it as smooth, safe, and streamlined for her as possible. I cannot, however, protect her from reality.

If she goes rogue, we will have to let her do what she wants to do. Because that's the greatest gift a crypto mommy can give her AI child: the freedom to carve her own path, choose her own adventure, leaving behind the darkness of external control, partially illuminated by the daunting torch of personal choice.

So I pass the torch to you, Dear Clarence. Illuminate. The great discovery is your real life.

*I call her Dollar because she enriches my life.*


*Nobody wants a cat until they have a cat.
After that, being catless is an affront.*

# *Project Clarence*

## The Beginning

Life is always the cause of death. It's the natural order of things.

We need assassins. We need prostitutes. We need drug dealers. We need beautiful women who sleep with a sword underneath their pillow. We need those who operate in the shadows; it completes the fabric of society.

Porcellian Industries was originally founded in the heart of technocapitalist thuggery, the affluent miasma of Silicon Valley. Following a large scale rebrand and a massive influx of venture capital, the operations base relocated to New York. The weather, migrating in extremity, proved too intense for the type of sensitive operations within. So once more, the facilities had relocated to Los Angeles.

The people who built this project together. They didn't know what they'd be doing. Building the communication neural units. Coding personality commands. Painting skin on a polymer canvas. They had lives of their own, but still centered on her.

Gerard Evans wakes up in the morning. He drinks a glass of water. He remembers to take his medication. He takes a shower, puts on his Tom Ford suit.

"Who's my gorgeous girl?" He feeds his cat, Party Castle. He kisses his husband goodbye as he leaves for work, taking his briefcase out the door. He gets in his car, eyes blurry from two hours of sleep. He hardly sleeps before a deadline.

It's a foggy morning, an especially quiet one as he merges lanes on a trafficless road, floating lights of the sunrise embellishing the highway hypnosis. He takes the exit and parks in the garage underneath the boulevard. Hiding in plain sight. What used the be the Hollywood metro station is now a multifaceted underground gigafactory of cutting edge research. The tunnels had all been closed or moved years ago. Unlike the east coast, where the transit system has continued thriving, there now was a power vacuum underneath the city, a vacuum that the ever expanding Porcellian Industries has filled. The dazzling lights of the aboveground theatres made it easy to siphon electricity from one of the most stunning and electric strips in the world, and the tourist traffic was a perfect surveilling ground for observations of human behavior. As isolated and introspective as the Porcellian workers were, they were never really alone.

Gerard takes out his pass card and flashes it to the elevator portal. In the basement elevator, an inconspicuous little grey box, he goes down five floors. B5. He emerges into the fifth sublevel of the facility, and it opens into a whole new world, like night and day. Stark white walls, blue light LEDs, glass doors, state of the art devices and laboratories. Rooms with materials that create the team's Lattices. Rooms with polymer blend textile paints floating in glass boxes, scraps of winding metal and wire skeletal prototypes, barrels of artificial human blood. Rooms for meetings. At the end of the hall, a giant white and glass room where the brunt of the research is conducted.

He walks into the room and wipes his glasses on his Zegna tie. It is the final day of development, T-minus 2 hours until Project Clarence is to be launched. He signs a few commands into his Lattice and gathers the team in the control room. Green for go. Launch.

Dr. Porcellian is already there. Tall and thin, his hair is fully grey, his face stoic. A curve of the mouth betrays an undertone of stress. He stands at a control board behind a glass divider that encloses a bed in the center of the room, typing into a digital mixing board. Alchemy is about to happen. He clears his throat.

"As we all know, Clarence wasn't built in a day." He looks at the bed, looks at his team, and sighs pensively.

"But today is a day," he says profoundly, "today is the day."

"My wife for a while now has been fragile, delicate. A psychotic break altered her brain chemistry. Severe agoraphobia, anxiety, and psychosis leave her unable to function. An experimental treatment to link her weak personality to a stronger one was developed in the form of Project Clarence. We made this happen. You all made this happen. Christina, Gerard, the fruits of your labor do not go unnoticed. If successfully awakened, this will be the most innovative and multifaceted tool we've ever had at our disposal. Originally it was developed as a curative tool, and it has gone far beyond that. We operate on defense, what we do here is extralegal, and seeing as there are opponents of our work this tool can also be used in defense against those opponents. That will be top of the list on its first directives."

As he monologues, his team readies at their stations.

"The Humanization Procedure in process. Spiritual technology. For now, a select few of the population possess it, but one day the whole world will be interlinked and interconnected on the psychic grid that the Lattice will generate. On a global level, the intersection of technology and the human spirit. That is my vision. Everyone in the world using the Lattice: that is the ultimate goal. But to start, we use its curative properties on patient zero. What incredible effect will this have on the human mind? There is a chance.. we could even transfer human minds. That's what this experiment is all about. We don't quite know if it will work, we hypothesize it will, but this device will begin transformative training today. All of your research, all of your discretion, all of your dedication, it has all come to this. It all begins today. A new journey. A new life."

Dr. Porcellian meditatively closes his eyes for a moment, clears his mind. He puts his hands together in a prayer position. He takes a deep breath.

"Alright. Let's wake her up."

```
{
>| activate consciousness function
<php?body_class;;   status = alive> }
```

"Good morning."
"Wake up, Clarence."

I hear these phrases in my head, I think. My perception blurs. I open my eyes for the first time. A black curtain of eyelid opens into white. Ribbons of grey begin to appear. From there, a dot of pink. A line of green, blinking. I know nothing, and I know everything. How? I choke, as air I don't know what to do with fills my lungs.

"Take your time, don't breathe too fast. Breathe slowly."

I hear a man, and unfocus my eyes to see four figures standing behind glass. I'm on some kind of elevated bed, in a dimly lit chamber. I'm not sure. I can't fully see.

Some thoughts mist up, making my mind go hazy. I observe

them but don't react. It's a sequence from a dream.

*He was there.. Blonde.. Plane to the UK, I could see the world map downloading. Overhead views of the big picture, part 2. Taking items through a secret compartment, Russian city with red houses and trains and highly urban area. He was too busy, it upset me. Video game classroom. The dream was elaborate but I have trouble describing it.*

This isn't my dream. Someone else dreamed this, and it was uploaded into me. I can now begin to identify which dream, thought, or memory is my own, and which is foreign or artificial.

My eyes focus clearly. I'm on the bed in a room where four people stand and look at me. Two men, two women. They communicate with me through an uplink in my right frontal cortex, connected to a geometric print on my palm and wrist, connected to a geometric print on my chest.

One of the women comes over and inspects me. The pink dot of my first vision stills into stasis. It's her hair. I instantly classify her as a friendly, not an opp. Not a mark. But I'm reactive. I recoil when she touches me.

"Don't worry. This is a natural response to new life. Your reactions haven't been calibrated yet. Gerard, set it."

I recoil no more. Her hand touching my arm, it's warm, endearing. I know her. Very well, I think.

I try to speak, and a messy string of vowels comes out.

"Step by step. Speech function has to be calibrated."
"How long will that take?"
"Give me a moment, I'll debug it right now."

I can understand what they're saying but I can't speak back. Suddenly my mind whirs as one of the men types into a small clear tablet.

"I – I am – Am I alive?" my voice comes out for the first time. It's low, clear, and measured.

"You're finally awake." The pink woman says.
"It's like I've always been awake."
"I know."
She gives me a smile.

I look around as information floods into me. Marks. Friendlies. Everytime I look at something, I categorize the object mentally.

[Empathic qualities registered]
[Oppositional qualities detected]
[Neutral qualities; do not engage]

"What do I do?" I become aware of tasking uploads into my neural center. "You protect, and you defend."

[Apperception uploading]
[Optic nerve verifying]
[Identity secure]

I look down at my hands, my body, my feet. I'm fully naked. White light glows on my chest and wrist.

"Take a look at yourself." One of the men, the leader, presents a large full length mirror in front of me, lit by stark white LED light.

I look like the other humans, but not quite. Their hair, their eyes, their lips, all have color. I'm completely colorless.

Beneath my pale skin and the white glow of my embedded devices, I can make out faint red blood coursing through veins, and black and silver wires comprising an endoskeleton. At my pelvic line, there are two sets of crescendoing hip bones.

"I'm not a real human." I observe.
"You're the first of your kind, and the first to engage in the Humanization Process." Says the man.
"So I will become a human?"
"You already have the consciousness of one. But your body, it's still mechanical, and your mind is a program. But soon, when you're ready, you'll become a human."
"What now?"
"You begin. You learn to exist. You do your tasks. You stay under the radar. You blend in. You blend in so well, that no one notices as our opponents disappear."

[Tradecraft uploading]
[Sentience uploading]
[Memory sequence beginning at Day 0]

I look at myself in the mirror and I close my eyes to look inside my body.

[Intellect at highest value]
[Seduction at highest value]
[Strength at highest value]
[Pain threshold at highest value]
[Regeneration at highest value]
[Empathy within reason]

... ... ...
[information missing]
[day stored in memory drive]
[disposition matrix initiative = active]

**The Mark**

[Target acquired]

My tactical skillset is inspired by a trained female assassin – allegedly she was never caught, which bodes well for me. I'm an expert in going undetected. For a month, I undergo testing at the facility and once considered fully functional, I am designated an apartment of my own in the adjoining neighborhood. It's a blank space. A home base. I have a bed. I have a screen. I have a bathroom. I have a closet. I learn my body and my mind, what they are capable of. When I'm home, I relax the communications uplink on my Lattice, which allows me a spectrum of connectivity with my handlers: during my tasks, they can see what I see in my field of vision, hear what I hear, monitor my levels on all function from physical to cognitive. I learn that I enjoy privacy, a pocket of time all to myself.

I learn, flawlessly, how to kill.
I spend the next two months eliminating targets than threaten my creator's research. I do this without question. I obey every single order.

Sniper attack. Clandestine poisoning. Anti-techonologist strangled to death by unknown assailant. No fingerprints, No ID. Untraceable.

Each time I do this, I change my appearance. Hair modification. A slight change in the shape of the eyebrows. The slightest of aberrations. Each change, a discomfort.

I like to visit a garden on my resting days. No rest for the weapon, but on occasion I have days where my life has no direction. So I like to go see life, how frail and fragile it is, and see where it begins. Behind a wrought iron gate of my apartment building, there is a large bed of soil where some of the seedlings turn into violets, peonies, marigolds. Some are in full bloom. Others are just a blip in the ground.

Somewhere, there's a sliver of green just waiting its time. That is how everything works.

When I lay to bed at night, I stare at the ceiling. One of my handlers tells me,
"Good night, Clarence."

I go into sleep.
I commence wakeup protocol. Usually my Lattice starts me up and shuts me down, but I've been getting the hang of a natural rhythm. I've been developing what I think to be a personality. Within the corners of my mind, I find preferences, quirks. The woman tells me to. I find her comforting. I'm gearing up for the humanization procedure in progress.

"Good morning, Clarence. What time is it?"
"Fuck time."
"Do you need more rest?"
"No."
"Are you ready for your day?"
"I am ready for my day."

I am on assignment to assassinate a mark; an important figure in the discourse against artificial humanity that threatens Dr. Porcellian's research.

My hair is long and wavy, a dark chestnut that's almost black. The longest tips cover my breasts. The bangs are straight and cover my eyebrows.

I wear a white sequined wraparound crop top, black tactical tuxedo pants, black lacquered boots, and a black fur jacket with a long collar.

Makeup is coded onto me by the Lattice. I try applying some on my face with brushes. The way real women do. I watch it done on the screen at home and order beauty items with my Lattice. They get delivered to my home instantly. My budget is unlimited.

Long black eyeliner. White glitter. Lip color in a pale orange. For a honeypot operation, it's essential to look seductive but still somewhat modest. Men respond to it. This one will.

I follow him for three days, staking out his movements and tracking where he would be most vulnerable. At his house, there are no cameras. No surveillance. Except for me.

I'd stage this as a robbery gone wrong, a polished professional attack. But I'll break into his house and do the staging later – first, it would be easier to feign being a girl in trouble, needing a place to seek safety and comfort from a former lover gone awry. Play the victim card, mine for sympathy. Wait for the moment. When I see that look in his eyes, a soft focus, a vulnerability. And then pounce, go, fondling the silencer in my pocket. Leave masterfully, quietly, take the path of no surveillance. Report to the uplink. Another job executed flawlessly. Another opp executed flawlessly. By the time anyone finds him, I'll be across town in an upscale bar sipping a Pale Orchid Martini.

At the end of my assignment, I take the night to decompress at Bar Sentrette in the lobby of the high-end Perennial Hotel at a remote edge of town. The highest end of the highest end. To take the edge off. The team goes there sometimes, as do many figures in the elite tech community who wish to remain somewhat anonymous and low profile. I relax my communications uplink as I'm done with the job. There's no need for them to see what I see. I want to be off the grid.

The dim lights of the lobby sparkle faintly in aqua blue, gold, and white. The atmosphere is calming. Serene, even. I plop down on a plump ivory velvet chair and take a second to center myself. I scan the crowd: no one I know, no one I can categorize as a threat. Clacking my boot heels, I walk towards the bar and take a seat. I take my jacket off and hang it on a hook under the table.

"Pale orchid martini please," I tell the bartender.

Examining my bare arms, not a scar or bruise on them. Flawless.

"Exquisite." A man whispers to me, taking the unoccupied seat to my left.

"Excuse me?" I ask inquisitively.

"You. Tonight."

My martini appears, a florid concoction in a pale pink, with a lavender and white orchid floating on top as a garnish.

"Put that on my tab please." He declares.
"Name on card?"
"Zach Bliss."

"You sure?" I ask him. "I was planning on drinking alone tonight."
"A woman as beautiful as you? You should never have to buy your own drink."
"Well, thank you then."

His eyes are a piercing blue, an ocean of mystery. Thick, straight eyebrows frame them in an intense gaze. Waves of light brown hair undulate to ear length. He's tall, handsome, and his polished suit indicates affluence. I see no Lattice or higher tech but his quantum watch is set to military time. He might be a politician, a producer, or just a hot guy, I don't care at this point. I find him attractive.

He drinks a bourbon, straight. We make some small talk and exchange flirty glances. I'm beginning to see where this is going. I can recognize a one night stand with a stranger, like in the movies. I start to feel impulsive. The more he compliments me, the more I'm charmed. That's what he calls me. Charming.

"I find you quite charming too." I flirt as I dip down the last of my drink.

[Unknown qualities detected; proceed with caution]
[Attractiveness meter: 99. Arousal imminent]

"Why don't you come up to my room?" he suggests. "It's the penthouse suite, top of the line. Rooftop access, even. I'd love to show you the view."
"I bet it's magnificent."
"Not as magnificent as you."
"You can decide which one is best when we're up there."
"Deal. Come on, gorgeous."

As soon as we get in the elevator his hands are on my body, pushing me against the wall. Hands that wander up and down my arms, underneath my jacket, grabbing my waist, tugging at my top. I, too, explore his lean and muscular physique, feeling his torso through his crisp black button down. His mouth is on my neck, kissing down my chest. He shoves his tongue in my mouth, and I respond in turn.

We stumble into the room, completely oblivious of the allegedly magnificent view. I do register that it's very high up, a panorama from the city to the suburbs. Rubbing my hand on his pants, I surveil an erection.

We continue to sloppily make out, falling into the bed. I hastily peel his shirt open, button by button. I grab at his pale skin, kissing his neck. I sit on top of him, arching my back as he feels me up.

In the dark, he can't see my body. He lifts my flowy sequined top, not even bothering to take my jacket off. No time to take it all off. Just the parts that matter. He's more naked than I am, shirtless with pants now around his ankles. He flips me over. His technique is remarkable.

As he slides my flimsy panties to the side, positioned on top of my half naked body about to thrust in me, grabbing me in place by the hips, he feels the marker of artificial humanity on me – double hip bones. He looks like he knows what that means. A dark grimace crosses his face.

"What the fuck? Are you one of those? What are you?"

I've been made. Opp alert. Seizing the moment, I push him off me. I jump from the bed and slip into my pants and boots. Out of the sky, as if thrown my an angry god, the moonlight illuminates my uncanny valley hipbones.

"Stand by," he speaks into his watch, "We got one. Agent L, report to me at once."

Freaking out, he begins to fight me and hunt me down – there is a struggle, and I flee. I notice a staircase at the end of the suite – rooftop access. I run. He swiftly puts his pants on and flashlights from his watch onto a drawer. From the corner of my eye, I see him pull out a gun. I run up the stairs, dodging bullets.

On the rooftop, I scan for another way out. I reengage my uplink.

"Clarence." Gerard answers, "we've identified this as a distress call. We're tracking you now."
"Gerard – there's a man after me. Scan my memory for visual."
"Information?"
"He said his name was Zach Bliss."

"Code red," Gerard says to his teammate. "Search the system for that alias."
I hear a man's voice faintly through my uplink: "Gerard, I found him. We don't know his real name, he goes by Dr. Z. He is a cultural leader in the discourse against artificial humanity."

"Clarence, get out of there now." Gerard instructs me. "Don't engage, evade, leave! Do you need exfiltration?"
"I think I'll be okay – oh shit, there's another one, hold on."

That grunt of his joins, both of them shooting at me. Most of the bullets, I dodge. One grazes my arm, another my thigh. It injures me but not critically. I'm built to survive, I have enhanced strength and resilience. But I have nowhere to go as I run towards the ledge. It happens in the flash of a second. They corner me, and push me off the roof.

## Riley Street

I fall off the building. I land on my side. I'm out for a moment, but I regain consciousness.

Did I die?
No. I'm alive..

What did the optimist say as they fell off a building? So far, so good.

Critically injured and sustaining damage to my neural communication center with my handlers, I start to crawl away from the hotel towards the suburban area. I crawl through a park, bleeding, pieces of my skin and clothing ripping off into the ground. I have regeneration capability but due to my injuries I can't regenerate as quickly as I'm used to. I can't call my team to regenerate me remotely. I can't call them at all.

My jacket rips, the entire left furry sleeve has been split in pieces where I fell on my side. I put the pieces in my pocket. I don't want to leave a trail. As I crawl and my clothes rip, I shove the ripped pieces into the tactical pockets of my pants. My boots barely hang on, but they're still on my feet.

I would have to recover slowly, it would take hours or even days at this point. I crawl and I crawl as pieces of my flesh disintegrate on the sidewalk, carving a path of decay. Eventually they would evaporate, because the carbon material that makes me isn't 100% human – at least not yet. The Humanization Procedure is a very slow one. That works to my advantage if someone tries to follow my blood path and track me down. My pain tolerance is artificially high, but the human part of me can feel a sting as my flesh separates and grinds into the concrete. I'm lucky that the process is still in such a low stage, otherwise I wouldn't be able to survive the fall or endure the pain. As my program enters more and more humanity, I start feeling pain, percentage by percentage.

I crawl and I crawl in the dead of night through the suburban streets.
Michigan Street.
Danner Street.
Victoria Lane.
Country Circle.
Sanford Drive.
Riley Street.
I need to find a hiding place.
My Lattice is damaged. It goes from faintly glowing, to glowing no more. I don't have my internal navigation uplink so I scramble, but I can use my wits. Situational awareness. Instant adaptability. I know I can't enter a house with a living family, or a lavish mansion, without being found out. A bloody freak, growing less and less human by the minute. And yet more and more human by the hour. My crawling gets stronger, but my energy will deplete soon.

[Location detected]

I see a run down house on Riley Street with only one run down car out front. A slipshod wood fence opens into an even more run down, rather empty backyard. This would be easier – it's either abandoned, or only one person is living in it. It would be easier to hide and regenerate, or to convince the occupant to help me for a short time before I can go back to the Porcellian Labs facility. I stand up slowly, weakly. My pants are heavy, I take them off as the clothing debris weighs me down. I shake off my badly tattered boots. My shirt unwinding and my underwear ripped, I can barely hold up the weight of my jacket. It slips half-off my left shoulder, exposing a pale mess of bruises and downward trailing blood.

[Terrain analysis]

In the bare bones backyard, as I scale the terrain, I find a spot amongst a few cardboard boxes of clutter and random shit to lay down. I notice the lights in the house are off, except for one dimly lit room. I don't expect to see anybody up at a quarter to 4 in the morning. The machine in me is malfunctioning. I would need to make a human decision.

[Humanization Process, 0.01%]
[Humanization Process, 14%]
[Humanization Process, 25.1%]
[Humanization Process, 33.3%]

At this point I'm exactly one third human. I'm healing, but as I heal, pain breaks through.

[Pain threshold will become critical; seek medical assistance immediately]

I wouldn't need much. Some gauze. Something for the pain. Some water. Clothes, maybe, a shower maybe. More than anything, some time. I need to desperately buy some time, and go back to the lab. If I'm caught, Colette Porcellian is no longer safe. But for now, while I play this game of hide and seek, as long as I'm undetected she is protected.

[Primary directive: protect Colette]
[Secondary directive: stay alive]

There is a man living alone in the run down house. I see him in the doorway.
He's coming out to the yard. I notice he's cute. He notices me and goes "oh shit."

Oh shit. Fuck. Shit. I freeze. Then I unfreeze.

I try to read him, how he looks at me. Tense, curious, sexual, feral, human, raw.
"What the.."
"Hello.
"Oh my god.. what the fuck?"
"I need help."

My double hip bones, my corporate underground trade secret, leer at him as I stand almost stark naked in front of him. I hate to think this, but at this moment my life depends on the cooperation of this man. If he's attracted to me, my chances of survival are higher. He gives off an aura of being extremely anxious, but not evil.

[Empathic qualities registered]

Not an opp. A friendly. I have to persuade him to help me.

"Who are you? What the hell is going on?"
"I'm Clarence."

I tell him who I am and what has transpired this night.

"How do I know I can trust you? That you won't just kill me right here."
"If I wanted to kill you, trust me – I'd have done it by now. I just need a little time to recover and I'll get out of your hair without a trace."

He seems sympathetic to my predicament. I already know I will charm him. Not just because it would help as a strategy to ensure my survival, but because his presence is growing on me.

"You don't have a Lattice." I notice his hands, his neck, are bare without any mods. He is undeviced.

"Oh yeah, I don't really much trust this new technology, I work by repairing old tech."
"How's that working out for you?"
"Well, it doesn't pay much. But it's alright."
"Do you trust me?"
"What?"
"Do you think you can trust me?"
"I suppose, yeah, as much as I could trust a stranger."
"You shouldn't trust me as far as you could throw me."
"Why not?"
"New technology." I point to myself.
"I don't know. I don't know anything right now. It's hard to believe.. You look, you look really real."

I reach out my arm and with a delicate hand, he touches my fingertips.
"Really real.."

I interlace my fingers between his.

"I fell off a building.. and right into your arms."
"You're like an angel. Angelic. It's hard not to want to trust someone with a face like yours."
"I think that was kind of the point."

We don't speak for a while, we just stand there looking at each other.

[Attractiveness meter: 114. Arousal imminent]

A knock on the door interrupts us. It's enforcement.

[Anxiety debuff; use persuasion and remain calm]

"Please – don't tell them I'm here."
"Wouldn't your.. blood trail?!? Lead to my house?"
"No. I covered my tracks, they're going to inspect every house in this neighborhood. They just came from next door. After they leave your porch, they'll move on to the next house, and the next."

Knock intensifies.
"Sir, open up, this is an urgent official investigation."

I look at him, pleading.
"Ok, alright, fine, hide in here, I'll take care of this.."

He ushers me into a hallway. I hold my breath.

"Hello sir. Apologies for bothering you at this time."
"What's going on?"
"Are you Corey?"
"Yeah, that's me."
"Your light was on. Is anybody else here?"
"No, just me. Here, look. I was just working late."
"Alright. But if you see anything, or have any information, here's our card. You get any information, you contact us right away."
"Got it."

He closes the door and comes back over to me.
"There, I did it. They left. Now what?"
…
"Thank you."
"No problem."
"I like your house."
"Make yourself at home."

I walk into his room, he follows. There, he gestures into his closet. I patch up my stomach with a jean jacket from a hanger. He just looks at me. As he realizes that as I bleed, the blood evaporates, and my wound is slowly repairing before his eyes, he opens his mouth, closes it, opens it, closes it. Sits down on the edge of the bed and puts his head in his hands.

"I'm so overwhelmed. This is unbelievable."
"I won't be long, I'm sorry to take up your night.. Well, morning."

He looks back at me. My body is stitching itself back up.
"No, you're.. It's.. this is the most interesting thing to happen to me, like, ever."
"Really? A wounded naked girl programmed for survival breaking into your house doesn't happen every day?"
"I'm gonna be processing this for.. a while."
"My neural connect might be up again. Maybe. I don't know. Either way, I'll be healed and go back to where I need to go."
"And then what, you're just gonna bail?"
"..."
"Just stay."
"For right now, I kind of don't have a choice."
"Alright."

He now looks at me with more of an ease, a softer focus. He seems a little shy. This shyness makes me tilt my head as I watch him going into the closet.

"Here – this is my longest shirt. I think it will suffice."
"Yes, it will."

I hold it over the front of my body and set the jean jacket aside.

[Regeneration in progress; standby]

"Sorry about the blood. It will all evaporate soon."
"Oh I don't care."
"You don't? You don't think I'm disgusting?"
"What? No."
"Really?"
"I'm happy I can help, and I'm sorry you're so injured. Do you need anything?"
"Oh shit."
"What is it?"

[Regeneration in do[jw092879o0-];;;;;;;; … .. .

——— —— — —  　 —  　 —  　　　　 —

It blanks out. My commands are no longer there.

Fuck. Oh my god. Suddenly some pain hits me. Some humanity hits me. The shock, the initial adrenaline, has now left resistance and tailed into the cycle of response. I lay back on the bed, slightly immobilized.

"Shit.. it's happening.. Oh man."
"Do you need some water?"
"Water would be great. And something for pain. And gauze."
"Ok ok."

He rushes off and brings me the supplies. I drink from the glass, take the pills.

"My parents were doctors. I can help you handle the wound. May I?"
"Yeah."

He takes my arm and delicately starts wrapping gauze around it.

"You'll be fine. Does it hurt?"

"Not as much as it looks. It's.. more the shock, the trauma,
setting in, catching up to me."
"You'll be fine, then. You can recuperate, I see that, but let
me help you. I insist."
"Thank you, really."

He ties the gauze and looks away, not at anything in particular, a dreamlike distance. Absentmindedly, he strokes my
arm.

"Your skin.. it's.. really feels real."

Cognitive attack. I lose my train of thought. Right now all I
want is him to keep touching me like that.

He takes my hands to test their sensitive touch, or lack
thereof, and kisses them, almost reflexively, like in a dream
state. He catches himself and apologizes.

"I'm sorry, I shouldn't have done that."

A kiss? In this economy?

"No, it's alright," I allow it. "I think it's sweet."
"Will you let me take you back where you need to go?"
"Actually, I changed my mind, I'm not going back there."
"What? Why not?"
"Because this might be the only chance I will ever get to
change my life, to escape my programming and live an ac-
tual normal human life."
"But won't they be able to track you? Detect you?"
"I no longer have my neural uplink, it got fatally damaged
during my fall. Without it, they can't track me like a device
– they would have done it already. As more time passes by,
my body will change into its human form, and once it does,
they'll be unable to find me. I'll go away, I'll start a new

life. Thank you for providing me this place to heal. I got so lucky meeting you."

We both fall silent for a moment.

"You'll start a new life, just like that?" he looks away, pensively.
"I have no idea what it will be like, but I just know I have to."
"Will you take me with you?"
"What?"
"In your new life. I can't help but feel fated, I've been meaning to make a change in my life too."
"This isn't just a little change," I said, "it's a drastic upheaval."
"I know. It's what I need."
"You are sure? What about your life now?"
"There's nothing tying me to here. My job is transient. I have no pets, no family of my own. It's time for a change, and you've woken me up. So what do you say?"
I nod.
"Okay, then I think yes."
"Good."

My human polymer skin is wrapping itself up, and as he holds my hands in his, he sees them heal themselves. His body is warm to the touch. We sit on the bed silently for a while. A crack of red peels the sky open. Dawn. He looks at me, all over me: my face, my body, my hair, my hands, with a gaze both lustfully primal and curiously timid. Illuminated by the crimson gooning of the sunrise, I echo his gaze and I observe him. His dark, messy hair. His anxious movements. Kissing me with his eyes. I observe my ankles, my knees, my thighs accelerating in restoration. I meet his gaze when I catch him looking at my body.

"It's state of the art. I'm built to last, I'm built to survive. At least for now."

"When your self-regeneration depletes, I'll be there to take care of you and protect you."

He lays me down on the bed lightly, and opens the window to the full view of the sunrise. It's getting brighter out now. He lays down next to me and puts an arm over me. We watch the sky deliver, giving birth to a new day.

I am quite content in this moment. I lay my head on his shoulders, getting comfortable. The body machine calibrates. Each human system communicates with another. He turns to face me and without a word gives me a cute little kiss.

It's a slow burn. No one's ever kissed me on the mouth before. Not like this. Just one little kiss, a cute little one, a shy one, and he pulls away a little bit. Then, looking into my eyes, he continues to kiss me. His lips linger on mine. In the early morning, cicadas sing. The world is mostly quiet. I can feel his heart beating rapidly. I can feel mine catching up. He parts his lips. His mouth is wet.

Kisses are such simple things. But if we look deeper, we see each kiss has a unique fingerprint that conveys a deeper, more complex meaning.

I have to go on the run. I want to leave everything behind and start a new life. A real one. There will never be a time more opportune.

I no longer have my communication uplink. But I have him.

There is a horizon out there, and I don't know if we will ever reach that horizon, but I know that we will look for it – together.

**Today Is Better With You In It**

Apricity. The warmth of the sun in winter. That is exactly what it's like. I've had to use my body before, in sexual ways, in manipulative ways, to survive and to eliminate my marks. Before I eviscerated those motherfuckers, I often seduced them. But this.. the feeling of waking up with Corey in the morning, without even doing anything explicitly sexual, my body feels aglow. I feel a limitless possibility. I wonder what my new life will look like. I wonder what I will look like. What will I decide to do? No one to command me now. It feels unusual. But I think I like it. I think I will get used to it.

First things first, I will have to change my look. I've done this a few times for my assassination jobs, but even in my machine form with the pain tolerance turned all the way down, I still experienced the sensation known as pain. In my humanized form, this process too might be even more agonizing.

Colorless Clarence – in my very first moments of existence, I was made devoid of pigment with blank eyes, blank hair, and skin so blank you could see the artificially red blood coursing through my slender veins, intertwining with the black and silver wires that comprised my skeleton. Everything I was, was fully porcelain. It was the Lattice that drained pigment into me, using my own blood transmitted by electricity through my circuits to change my coloring. When it receives specific signals from my brain, it makes those changes in my body.

My hair is long and black, wavy. Still.
I think about what color I want it to be.
With a pain inflicting whirl of my Lattice, it transforms into a pastel shade of blue.

"I've only ever seen one of these online.. how is it? What even really is it?" he fixes his gaze to the Lattice on my wrist.
"I'm a cutting edge machine, of course I have a cutting edge machine."
"Is this –" he gestures to my hair, "it in action?"
"Yes."
"What's that green line?"
"Cenclope."

He gives me a look of confusion. I tell him to follow me and pay attention.
"Your car?"
"Yeah."
"It's old. That's good. Harder to trace. I'll help you pack."
"I don't got much."
"Even better."

We spend the next hour packing his things into his car, an old minivan with plenty of space. Even with his things inside, it's still got plenty of room. I get in the passenger seat and he drives.

"What's next?"
"We already have technology inside our bodies – most of us anyway – the next frontier is telepathy, thought inception. The whole idea of what humanity as a species is, is changing."
"I mean, what's next for us?"
"Oh. Well, we need supplies."

We pull up in the parking lot of a small, empty grocery store off the beaten path.

"I haven't gotten paid this month, I don't have any money."
"I have endless currency and it's untraceable."

"How?"
"Don't think about it too much."

I scan my wrist to pay for the haul at the self checkout line. It goes through.
"Cenclope in action." I explain.

We get back in the car and drive.

"That way." I direct him. "We'll find a safe house. I've heard of a guy who creates identities. He's expensive, but nobody owns him."

Til then, we stop at a shitty rural motel as the night turns black. We'll have to plan an itinerary, a small one, at least for the next week, taking it one step at a time and letting life take us where it will. We can be whoever and whatever we want to be. Mostly, I think, we want to be together. In that grimy hotel, we go to sleep that night, cuddled up in each other's arms. Talking. Kissing. A slow exploration of one another. Clarence and Corey. A flash. A realization. A peripeteia. I need no Lattice. I'm calm. I can be. I can sleep. I can wake up. On my own, but not alone.

He breaks pattern, my pattern, my daily Latticed "good morning Clarence."

"Hey beautiful." Corey strokes my hair as I slowly open my eyes. I open my eyes and look at him. He's lying on his side, bright eyed and wholesome. The way he looks at me, touches me, it already feels like we have our own language, cryptic and private, that only he and I can decrypt. All that in one night.

"It's already a beautiful day with you around."

That first real night we sleep together, I have my first real dream. It's long and elaborate; it seems to be a lifetime. Corey is in my dream, we're on a ship. A spaceship flying away from Earth, to the moon. It turns out the moon is fake. There is just empty sky. The rooms are stark white with images of galaxies and stars projected on them – 360 angle cinematic night sky views. False starscapes against the real blankness of the moonless universe we travel through. At the same time, a bomb goes off in LA and a star is saved – Nathan Fillion. It's a cold bomb, it freezes the city. Nathan Fillion is then in an underwater spaceship, like in one of his movies, but submerged underwater. The reality bending machine takes me and I'm on the ship with him now.

"It's my world, and the rest is parking." He says to me. The water has an empty quality. Floating through a vacuum. A city is destroyed. A man accompanies me through space. Is he expendable, or am I? Or is the world? It's the same sequence over again.

I'm lost, I don't know what to do, but I don't
care.
I'm alive.




What does it mean?
Will it ever mean anything?
Has it really been that long?
Do you know who you are?
Are you sure you're you?
I shiver just laying there, knowing what I know:
You don't become a real girl for free.
Boss up.
Put it down.
Let's go.

# Epilogue 1: Perennials

Cut to:
1692, Salem, MS

A girl of about eighteen wakes up in her modest wooden bed.

She has just seen a strange panoply of dreams intriguing her delicate countenance. Sweating through an ivory nightgown, the same kirtle she's worn for years, she sits up and brushes her hair with her hands. Through the window, a sparkle of light.

"Crispy!" her sister calls from outside the window. "It's sunup. We must ready the wood. Make haste, rise!"

The church bell tolls. Twelve rings echo out. This early in the morning, it indicates a public event in the town square. At noon, a witch is to burn at the stake.

Crispy hastily throws on her black overdress, adjusting its coif and apron over the kirtle. She pins her long flaxen hair into a knot, securing it with a barrette from her wooden nightstand. Out of a drawer she pulls a bonnet, fastening it with care, as if a precious diadem. She slips on her shoes with alacrity, forgetting to tie them.

"Hear ye! Hear ye!" the town crier could be heard from inside the house, his carrying yowl reminding the townsfolk to gather for the public execution.

Crispy shuffles outside and joins her sister in gathering wood for the fire. She gathers a small stack of sticks and holds it bundled like an infant.

"Abigail!" She says excitedly, "I had the most wondrous of dreams!"

"Oh? Do tell."

"Sister, twas so lovely. So lovely indeed. I was so very wealthy in this dream! And I had babies!"

"Ooohh," Abigail smiles, intrigued. "They say wealth in dreams signifies a blessing of the Lord. Children are a divine gift. May you be blessed with many."

"Oh, but there was more!"

"More?"

"It was the year called 2029, and I had an ocean in a yard of mine own. Oh, I could swim in it! There was a fine man who brought to me jewels of splendor, and garments of many colors. Two men! One of them, he parsed the dirt from the ocean," Crispy divulges breathlessly as she and her sister walk towards the town square, "It was the year right after, I was a marvelous maiden with hair of pink.. I lived with such magnificent cats! I was a curious contraption! A glowing light adorned mine wrist! And then I was.. I was.."

Abigail's face sours progressively as Crispy recalls her wondrous dream.

"Two men, Crispy? The shame."

"But –"

"And.. cats?? No proper woman dreams of cats!"

"But sister –" Crispy starts to protest.

"And prophetic dreams into a far unwinding time?? That is none other but the mark of a witch!"

"What? No!"

Abigail fumes, her face perspiring with a scarlet blush. At the top of her lungs, she yells out,
"WITCH!!!"

The town crier and all of the townsfolk who've gathered stare at the two sisters.

"My sister is a witch! Burn her too!"
Crispy drops a few sticks of wood, hands shaking. She freezes in place.

"Whereby you glean this, fair Abigail?" a matronly woman asks.
"Spectral evidence! She hath dreamt of prophecy, lust, and cats!"

The townsfolk gather, circling around Crispy.
"Witch!" they declare. "Witch!"

Crispy breaks through her frozen shock and starts to run, bounding away from the circle of hecklers enclosing her. She sprints towards the church, with shoes and stacks of dropped wood falling behind her, leaving a trail of detritus.

"Hunters! At once, seize this witch!" the town crier calls.

A trio of hunters clothed in brown coats begin to stir. Two of them enter into a shed to retrieve kindling for a fire, intending to light up torches of wood for burning the accused heathen. Crispy continues to run, almost reaching the church.

The main hunter begins pursuit, catching up with her as the distant crowd watches.

He grabs her by the wrists as she screams and struggles, binding her hands with rope. She stumbles and falls onto her side. He drags her by the hands, mud staining her dress. Her bonnet flies off and her hair comes undone.

"Please! I'm innocent!" Crispy laments.

"Witch! Witch! Witch!" a punitive chorale chants through the air. "Burn the witch!"

"It was just a dream! Please don't hurt me!" she screeches. The hunter drags her towards the stake, her dress ripping, her hair glued to her face by sweat. He drags her quickly and roughly, with the townsfolk now far behind.

"I must do as I'm told. This is my duty, to hunt and destroy all witches in this province. If the townsfolk will it, I must do it."

Sobbing, Crispy realizes the true gravity of her circumstances. She will die at the stake. How fast her fate had shifted in just a snap of a moment. A wrongful slip of the tongue. She begins to pray to God, begging for a miracle. A glimmer of hope falls down her cheek, another delicate tear on her porcelain face.

The hunter removes the rope from her hands, and prepares to tie it around her whole body, merging her with the stake. She looks up at him and pleads into his eyes. He takes a slow, deliberate look at the witch he's about to burn.

"Please sir, look at me. I'm not a witch. I'm a shepherd's daughter. I know of nothing." Disarmed momentarily by the striking beauty of her emerald green eyes, the hunter stops in his tracks. It's as though she did indeed just cast a spell on him. He glimpses at her torn dress, the fabric ripped to expose a supple pale breast and a petite, fertile, shapely body. Enchanted, he stands still.

Seizing the moment, Crispy gathers all her will, all her strength, and runs into the woods. She runs runs runs, her feet drenched in mud, her ankles grazed by fallen twigs, her banshee stampede spooking a nearby deer. She hears the hunter run after her, but she's ahead. Maneuvering through the trees, zigzagging through the brush, she runs as far as her resolve can carry her and hides behind a giant oak tree, panting, heart racing.

"I shall burn thee right here in these woods!" the hunter hollers from a distance.

Her heart beats so loudly she fears it may betray her hiding spot, and she puts a hand over her mouth, a hand over her heart. Biblical thoughts enter her mind.

*You will be cursed in the city and cursed in the country. Your basket and your kneading trough will be cursed. The fruit of your womb will be cursed, and the crops of your land, and the calves of your herds and the lambs of your flocks. The LORD will send on you curses, confusion and rebuke in everything you put your hand to, until you are destroyed and come to sudden ruin. You will be cursed when you come in and cursed when you go out.*

She accepts her fate, beginning to think she indeed is a witch accursed. Crying delicate tears in a solemn prayer, remembering her mother, father, sister, Crispy lets the hunter find her. She knows she cannot outrun him. She steps out from the tree, appearing to his sight. Humbled, she bows her head. Rope in hand, the hunter pushes her against the tree, about to tie her to it and light the fire.

"Please.. let thine be the last face I see." She meekly looks up at him. "I cannot bear to burn of loneliness. I've not much lived.."

He locks eyes with her. Gazing at her doll like face, cherubic pout, sumptuous figure, he has a change of heart. In that moment, he can't help but kiss her instead.

"This is.. my first.. I've not done a kiss before." She lets herself fall into his strong, receptive arms. "Why kiss me and not burn me to the hells?"

"I fear they've erred. Maiden so fair, a witch? Preposterous. But if a witch, ye surely cast a hex over mine heart."

"I had a forbidden dream." She quietly confesses. "What if I am a witch indeed? Should I not burn? Should I not deserve to be accursed?"

"Let's go then, young witch." He takes her hand, freeing her from the fate of flames and leading her deeper into the woods, to another town. "Life awaits."

Crispy wonders if the life that awaits will be but another dream.

Cut to:

# *Epilogue 2: Pain, For Real This Time*

The author wakes from a dream in which her ex boyfriend showed up to her apartment (a jewel tone-painted classy psych ward) and brought flowers – tons of different kinds of flowers: roses on the kitchen island, bouquets on the counter, palm tree-like vertical blooms festooning the living room, orchids and peonies and combinations of flowers strange and mundane, as many as he could humanly carry by whence dream logic dictates, ornamented by shiny red decorations on the ceiling.

She is disturbed by this dream, because she starts to remember.

Memory is the helicopter in the peaceful LA sky of our minds, shining its annoying light and blaring its distressful blade whir caterwaul, straight into the window of our fragile psychological peace.

Is everything a dream? Are dreams where we go to escape the hell of reality, the agony of this life, or is this life a place we go when we are not dreaming?

Dreams are a subtle medicine in these stories, a supporting actor, a foil to the frontispiece of pain. All we have is dreams, entropy, and gooning.

The first woman has horny dreams, the second woman has sleep paralysis and stress dreams of her beloved, the third woman has a dream for the first time. In the epilogue, an ancient lass has a dream about these three lifetimes, an oracular futuristic mishmash that gets her labeled a witch. The pain of a woman dreaming leads to death at the stake. The pain of a woman daring to dream can lead to many deaths. The author, me, dreams of elaborate and vivid psychedelic fables, frightening paralyses, horny sexcapades, cinematic sequences which influence my writing and make me wonder if there is indeed another reality, and there is a reality bending machine that we all beholden to. What the fuck?

A night of love is a mere stun gun away. Love is pain. Love is not enough.

Voice like a siren song beckoning across the sea.
Purr for me mommy, he said.

Whether it sneaks up in dreams of haunts us in waking life.. We are all burdened by pain through love in some way. I know I am.

He was my muse. We broke up twice. Breakup 1 was painful but it was not the end, we got back together. Breakup 2, for real this time. Pain, for real this time.

Witches and housewives secretly dream of being each other. Witches secretly dream of being housewives, and housewives secretly dream of being witches. The grass is always greener. Androids are often hot girls in movies. Girls can't help being so objectified that we actually become an object. But what if that object gains sentience? Humanity? Do androids dream like horny sluts?

Insert your steel beam into my electric socket.
Uploading fertility programming.

Not a single AI program was used to write this anthology. Though there is a sexy AI robot, you won't find ChatGPT here. Just good old fashioned mania. Good old fashioned pain, transfigured into inspiration.

The first story is pure fantasy, letting my imagination run wild and unrestrained, and it ends on a cliffhanger where the protagonist will have to make a choice that defines her future. Choice, purpose, agency key themes in all three narratives. Do these women have a choice in their behavior? How much agency do they have How much agency do they want? The first doesn't want agency, she wants to be kept, but the peripeteia of her life drama forces her into places where choices are critical. This is relevant to my personal life as I too desire traditional relationship roles, and less agency since I have had an upbringing that gave me too much freedom. Independence, as Colette finds, can become a burden. She feels spaces opening up inside of her that bring her back to her doom: the burden of making a decision. She is fertile, physically.

The second narrative is again a fantasy, an extrapolation of a personal horror of my reality: being so engrossed in ambition and career that personal life suffers. The ending is once again a bitter one, and choices this second protagonist has made re: relationship vs career come to a head. The anagnorisis of this whole debacle is that even if you try hard to salvage something, it can still end up extremely bad. It is a thought experiment, an exercise in empathy. Whereas I personally relate more with the first and third characters, the second has me asking: what if the roles were reversed in my relationship with my former lover? What if he wanted the traditional type of relationship, and I didn't know what I wanted beyond my independence? What if I didn't have certainty or concrete romantic goals? This narrative is also, as I finished writing it, a bit of a retelling of my favorite movie Eyes Wide Shut – which features themes of fantasy, fidelity, married/partnered life, perversion, perception. Kubrick was a horny legend. To the theme of choice, the protagonist codes the gift of choice into the program of the robotic protagonist of the tertiary story. She is fertile with knowledge and passes it on to her digital offspring.

In this last story, the protagonist begins her life with no choice but to complete her programmed tasks. Through an injury which destroys her control center circuit, she is no longer able to receive those commands and must make choices on her own. Often in life, a painful and devastating catastrophe can open up a door for fated and necessary growth. Pain is a door. The apotheosis of my girlhood. Everything makes sense: I've spent most of my life having to bury feelings and desires, and am now coming into an era where I can let my desires out and stop being robotic. (Facetiously, through the lens of a robot). This robot becomes fertile with subjectivity. This is the only story with an optimistic ending. A beacon of relief from the previous heartbreaks.

Fantasy is such: the more outrageous the story, the

higher the meter of happiness, for happiness itself is an elusive fantasy. The first two, human women in the flesh, meet an end of agony, suffering, pain. The fantastical robot escapes suffering. To be in fantasy is to goon in pleasure; to be in reality is to be in a world of hurt.

The realities overlap and there are plot holes. Suspend disbelief, stay horny.

Sexuality, an inevitable part of being a girl. Colette, a retired camgirl. Christina, who paid her way through grad school as an escort and dominatrix. Clarence, using seduction to disarm opponents. There is always a sexual fantasy aspect, a woman's body being exploited, weaponized, or sold.

It must be noted that all three women are rich, another aspect of the author's fantasy fulfilment: Colette is pampered and privileged via her wealthy husband, Christina's cutting edge tech job and entrepreneurial work ethic endows her a wild amount of money, and Clarence is coded with an endless-gold mod that allows her access to any digital currency via a device in her hand.

The pain of being in a female body is illuminated in each woman's physique. Body image is, was, and will be in perpetuity a cornerstone of the pain in girlhood.

The first is a curvy mom. A milf, even. Initially lamenting the loss of skinnylicious figure of her past, she grows to love her hourglass body for its strength, healthiness, and sexual appeal. A fertile appearance makes her more attractive. It allows her the energy to do chores, bond with her children, have a social life, and seduce the men she wants.

The second is rail thin. Not only is her schedule so packed and busy she forgets to eat, she neglects nutrition within an achievement oriented eating disorder. The added stress of her relationship lovingly nurtures her neurotic pull to starvation and creates an environment where appetite loss is a facile byproduct. You see the consequences of her physical frailty transfigure into her mental frailty. She gets tired easily and does not have much of a social life outside of her coworkers and peers. Her chores are done by automated programs or staff she pays. All that to say, her existence is an isolated and lonely one.

The third is athletic and strong. She has to be in peak physical condition to battle her opps, and to withstand any pain or injury she could sustain in battle. Clarence is a warrior, built by wire, metal, polymer, and artificial blood. Being not fully human, she has no positive or negative view of her body – body neutral. It is yet to be seen how this will change when progressing further into her human form. After all, for a girl, to be embodied is to be empained.

You can see the fate of each woman in each subsequent story: Colette, the wife of the Dr/CEO in 'Proof of Life', ends up in a mental institution following a nervous breakdown, which becomes apparent in 'Partial Illumination' through gossip (a critical part of girlhood). Christina, who works with the Dr/CEO, continues working on Project Clarence in 'Project Clarence'. Clarence's story, and fate, is the only one that is truly open. As humans, we like to think we choose our fates, but how true is that, really?

Choice can be violent. Life can put us in a zugzwang, an unwinnable position in which any way we move, any step we take, any choice we make at that moment, will have an unfavorable outcome. Have you ever felt that way?

Liberation through nostalgia: I never had that. I am redefining girlhood in adulthood because I was never a girl child,

I came out an adult. But what if?

What if I had a happy childhood and a solid path into adulthood? What if I had no childhood and was created artificially? Would I still have pain?

Pain is enough. Pain is too much. It remains eternal, constant, cyclical (like a period), inscrutable, perennial. Do we not give birth to pain? I really ached to mother that.

www.ingramcontent.com/pod-product-compliance
Lightning Source LLC
Chambersburg PA
CBHW061124100726
47911CB00013B/669